Barren

_____

By Stevie Turner

Title: Barren
Copyright © 2020 Stevie Turner
ISBN: 978-1838017156

Dedication

This book is dedicated to the father of my children.

Description:

Two mothers, but only one baby...

Esme Jones and husband Aron have completed their family and have twin sons Jared and James. Her older sister Eden Reece is desperate for a child, but a hysterectomy has put paid to any chance of her becoming a parent. Esme offers herself as a surrogate, and Eden and husband Billy are delighted. However, when Esme notices the first flutterings of life inside her and a scan reveals that she is carrying a girl, both sisters are not prepared for the eventual outcome when Esme realises baby Shannon is the daughter she thought she would never have. It is an outcome which threatens to tear the fabric of the whole extended family apart.

Table of Contents

Table of Contents

Part One, Chapter One
2007

At least it was all over now. Eden Reece shuffled slowly along the hospital corridor with her body supported in a vice-like grip by Billy's right arm. Her husband looked down at her with some consternation.

"Do you want to sit in a wheelchair?"

"No, it's okay." Eden shook her head. "We'll be there in a minute."

Eden knew Billy would not argue the toss; she would walk to the car under her own steam even if it took her the rest of the day.

"Don't forget, you're not supposed to lift anything for six weeks."

Instead of the tart response she would usually have made, she let Billy's gentle reminder wash over her like a rolling wave. The main entrance came into view, and she breathed a sigh of relief as she stepped out into the late June sunshine. A wall of heat lifted her sagging spirits at once.

"Where did you park?"

"Car Park A, just over there."

She followed the direction of his finger, and saw the unmistakable roof of their new red Ford Freestyle showing a few inches above other cars in the row.

"Let's get home."

In the past, he had only opened the passenger door for her if she had been carrying one of their precious embryos. Eden brushed away a tear. *One by one they had all failed except the lining of her uterus, which had flourished and continued to grow deep down into the muscular uterine wall. No babies would thrive there ever again. Somewhere not too far away in a laboratory jar, a stray pickled embryo might well have poked its head out of her formaldehyde-filled womb by now whilst calling out in a plaintive voice ... 'Mum!'*

She gave him a thin smile.

"Are you being a gentleman?"

"Trying to be." Billy gave her a wink. "I'm working on it."

***

She tried distraction therapy by sending Esme a text, but in reality felt every bump in the road even though Billy drove slower than usual. Eden, relieved at last to see their house come into view, managed a smile as Billy brought the SUV to a halt opposite the garden gate.

"Pleased to be home?"

"Yes." She nodded. "Definitely."

"Come on. Let's get you indoors."

Trying not to wince, Eden hobbled stiffly along the short path all the while musing on the fact that the last time she had walked out of the front door, her womb, ovaries and fallopian tubes had all been intact. She pushed away another steadying arm as she climbed onto the doorstep.

"Don't fuss, Billy. I'm all right."

The arm, unheeding of her instructions, came around again.

"You're wrapping me in cotton wool."

"'Cos I love ya." Billy gave her a quick peck on the cheek. "And I've got dinner all ready for tonight, as well."

The sudden coolness of the hallway made her shiver.

"Salad?"

"How did you guess?" Billy laughed. "Okay, I can't cook, but I can knock up an awesome salad. Go and sit down, and I'll bring you a cup of tea."

She felt as weak as a kitten. Eden sat down gingerly on the sofa and leaned back against a cushion. Fingers of afternoon sun filtered through the net curtain and illuminated her favourite photo above the mantelpiece; the two of them smiling on their wedding day eight years before. She felt tears sting the back of her eyes. *Who would have thought the diagnosis of adenomyosis would morph to cancer after a year and rob them of the chance of parenthood altogether?*

Her eyes moved along to the wall on the left, and focused on a ten year old canvas print of Esme and Aron laughing on their wedding day outside St. Mary's Church, Ipswich, whilst covered in confetti. Her sister, 31 and five years her junior, was already the mother of two adorable but boisterous twin boys. She, Eden, was an auntie, but although the twins were gorgeous and she loved them to bits, it was not the same as having a child of your own to care for.

Eden closed her eyes and imagined all the babies' faces that she would never carry inside her. Would they have had Billy's red hair, or her own mousey brown curls? Would they have been girls or boys?

"There's some lemon drizzle cake to go with it."

Billy's entrance brought her out from her reverie. Eden took the tea gratefully, and nibbled on the slice of cake. Billy sat down beside her and took her hand in his.

"All right?"

"Not really." She shrugged. "Life's bloody well not fair, is it?"

"You're alive". Billy gave her fingers a squeeze. "That's all that matters."

"I should have taken them up on their offer."

"What offer?" Billy looked at her. "Who?"

"The medics offered to freeze some of my eggs, but hey, I'm damaged. I didn't want any baby of mine possibly starting life with cancer."

Billy cradled both her hands in his.

"We've got each other. We'll be okay. You'll recover from this setback. Think of all the wonderful holidays we can have in the future without having to be stuck in children's playgrounds all the time."

She managed a thin smile.

"No sleepless nights. No shitty nappies. No photos in your wallet where your money used to be."

"That's the ticket." He brought her hands up to kiss them. "Who wants kids anyway?"

Eden leaned against him in silent thought.

Me.

She knew Billy, an only child, felt just as despairing in reality. They had planned for a big family in those heady early days of their marriage. What kind of wife was she that couldn't give her husband the baby they both wanted?

God played with her for reasons known only to *Him*.

Chapter Two

Esme Jones read another chapter from *George's Marvellous Medicine* whilst enjoying the warm weight of her eight year old twin boys as they leaned against each of her arms.

"We'll have another chapter tomorrow, but for now... bed!"

"But... Mum!" The twins cried in unison.

"No *buts*." Esme laughed. "I'll come up and tuck you in, and Daddy will be up in a minute to give you a kiss."

She burrowed her face into the top of each blond head before closing the book.

"Hurry up and get up those stairs and into bed before the bogey man comes!"

Squealing with delight, the two boys leapt from the sofa and raced each other to the top landing. Esme followed behind them more sedately and stuck her head over the upper bannister as she heard her husband come in from the garden.

"Aron! The boys have come up to bed!"

"Yeah...just coming, but I've got to wash my hands first."

Esme peeped out of the landing window. Aron had cut the back lawn and dug the flowerbed; not bad for one evening's work.

Each boy had climbed the ladder to his individual bed situated above an untidy desk full of toy cars, half-drawn pictures, and books mainly pertaining to robots and spaceships. They were now in the process of throwing soft toys at each other across the room accompanied by much giggling.

"Settle down!" Esme caught a bear as it sailed above her head. "I don't want to hear any more noise from the pair of you!" She climbed half way up the nearest ladder and squeezed the slight form hiding beneath the duvet.

"Love you, James." She peeled back the cover and planted a kiss on her son's cheek. "Don't let the bedbugs bite."

"Love you too, Mummy. I don't have bedbugs."

"That's good then."

She crossed the room to where Jared already had his arms outstretched. She grinned at him as she balanced on the ladder.

"Love you, Jared." She returned the hug. "See you in the morning."

"Love you too, Mummy." Jared yawned.

She passed Aron on the stairs and pinched his buttocks.

"Coming back this way?" Aron gave her a wink.

"I'll be in the garden. It's too nice an evening to sit indoors."

***

Heat radiated from the party wall of Norfolk flint pebbles running down one side of the patio. Esme let her hands rest briefly on the stones and then sank down into a deckchair, closed her eyes and listened to the birdsong. From the kitchen she could hear Aron as he rattled cups and saucers. There was a click as the kettle leapt into life.

"Oy, sleeping beauty. Fancy a cuppa?"

She turned her head and looked towards where Aron stood in the kitchen doorway, fair hair clipped in an identical brush-like style to the boys.

"Lovely!"

The church clock chimed eight o'clock. Aron appeared with two steaming cups, and handed one to Esme.

"Thanks, and the garden looks great by the way."

"All part of the service."

The evening sun seemed reluctant to set. They sat side by side and listened to the screams of neighbours' children protesting at the sudden ending of their day.

"At least ours go to bed fairly well." Aron pulled a face as a particularly shrill scream erupted from next door. "Although the little buggers will be giggling for a while I expect, about bodily functions and willies."

She chuckled.

"Talking about kids reminds me... Eden came home this afternoon. She sent me a message."

"Oh?" Aron looked at her. "How is she?"

"Not sure, but she did text to say they'd got it all and she didn't need any other treatment, just check-ups. I told her I'd phone tomorrow and have a chat. I thought I'd leave it today and let her get over it a bit."

Aron nodded.

"Good idea. Billy will look after her."

"Yes." Esme agreed. "But I know my sister. She'll keep everything to herself and won't talk to him about how she's feeling."

"Quite shitty, I should think." Aron replied. "Do you think they'll adopt?"

"Don't know." Esme shrugged. "They might be too old now. Billy's forty next year don't forget."

They sat in silence and drank their tea. An idea had formed in Esme's mind. She needed to speak to her sister. She picked up her phone and typed a text:

'Will Billy be at the yard tomorrow? If so, can I pop by about 10?'

There was an instant reply.

'*Yes, and yes.*'

***

Billy's van had gone. Esme rang the bell and waited a little longer than usual. Presently she was greeted by a slightly stooped over Eden, who appeared paler than usual.

"Hi Eden! You're looking well." Esme lied and gave her a hug. "Yeah, you don't look too bad at all."

"I feel like I've been run over by a tractor." Eden grimaced. "Come in."

Esme could tell her sister was in pain but putting on a brave face, as she followed behind her into the front room.

"I'll put the kettle on for some coffee." Esme announced. "You sit down."

"Thanks." Eden sat down gratefully. "I can't do much at the moment."

Esme rolled her eyes to the heavens.

"Of course you can't - you've just had a major operation!"

Everything in the kitchen looked clean and tidy. Esme set about making drinks. She carried a full tray in to the front room, and set it down on a small table between them.

"Did Billy make you some lunch?"

"Yes." Eden nodded. "It's in the fridge. He's gone to the yard."

Esme hesitated for a split second before speaking.

"Listen, I'm going to come to the point right away. I'm going to stick my neck out."

Eden paused bringing the cup to her lips.

"Don't worry. I'm not going to die just yet."

Esme shook her head.

"It's not that. It's about babies. I want to have one for you."

14

"What!" Eden sat up straighter. "Good God! No! I wouldn't ever dream of asking you!"

"You *haven't* asked." Esme looked her sister directly in the eyes. "I'm offering. As you know, Aron had the snip after the boys were born. He's puffing out powder as they say."

She was happy to see her comment raise a thin smile, and carried on.

"So our family is complete. You've tried for years to get pregnant. It's the least I can do for you."

"It's too big an ask." Eden shook her head. "And what would happen if you wanted to keep it after going all through the pregnancy? I bet you haven't even spoken to Aron about this!"

Esme leaned forwards in her seat.

"Not yet but I'm going to, *and* I wouldn't keep it. It would be yours and Billy's. By the way, I looked into the legal stuff online last night, and we can get a court order after the baby's here to register you and Billy as the legal parents if everybody agrees. I would have to register the birth to start with though as the legal mother, but I could state that your surname goes on the certificate."

"No. No. Bloody hell. No." Eden waved away Esme's comment. "It's not right."

Deflated, Esme sank back on the armchair.

"Okay. Have it your way. But... the offer's there, at least for the next five years. After that I'll be knocking on a bit."

Eden reached out a hand towards her sister.

"Thank you so much, but no."

***

Esme tried to shake off the deflated feeling when a good idea has gone bad. She had felt certain her sister would have jumped at the opportunity to be a mother, and could not understand why

Eden had put up so many barriers. Of course she, Esme, would not dream of keeping the baby! All she wanted to do was to make her sister happy. She decided to wait a while and then try again; perhaps when Eden felt better then she might change her mind.

Chapter Three

She had always hated the smell of old cars, oil and grease that hung around on him after a day in the yard. Eden waited until Billy was out of the shower, then made her way upstairs to the bathroom. She picked up his dirty overalls and put them in the laundry basket on the landing. Billy, naked and dripping, came towards her rubbing his hair dry with a towel.

"What about it then?"

"Er… yeah, but with the way I'm feeling at the moment… in about six months." She giggled.

He gave her a quick peck on the cheek.

"Don't go around picking up after me. You're supposed to be resting."

Eden leaned against the bannister thinking about how to word her next sentence, whilst admiring her husband's muscular frame.

"Nice pecs." She gave his backside a little slap as he made his way to the bedroom. "Listen…Ez came to see me today."

"Yeah?" Billy replied, half-heartedly.

"Yes. She wants to have a baby for us"

Billy ceased rubbing his hair. The towel dropped to the floor, and he turned to face her as she stood in the doorway.

"What?"

Eden smiled at him.

"I thought that would get your attention. Yes, she's offered to have a baby and then give it to us."

Billy picked up the towel.

"Bloody hell! What did *you* say?"

"I told her no" Eden replied with a shrug. "It's too much to ask somebody, even if she *is* my own sister."

Billy dressed himself in clean shorts and a tee shirt. He donned some crocs and looked at her thoughtfully.

"But she's willing…"

"What if she doesn't want to give it up?" Eden replied, her voice rising slightly. "That would be even worse!"

Billy shook his head.

"I know Ez. If she says she'll give it to you, then you'll have it."

"But how will …er…?"

Billy kept a straight face.

"Maybe Ez and I can go off for a romantic weekend together?"

"Over my dead body! It would have to be a syringe job."

"Sounds kinky." Billy guffawed. "What would I have to do?"

"Nothing. I'm not going through with it." Eden padded towards the top of the stairs. "It's just not right."

***

Eden shuffled over to Billy's side of the bed, where the warmth of his body permeated her own. An arm snaked around her shoulder as she cuddled up to his chest.

"Think about it." Billy kissed the top of her head. "We could be a family at last."

Eden shrugged.

"But it wouldn't be *my* baby. It's not ethically right. It would be yours and Esme's. Its mother would have to be its aunt. Poor little sod."

"Forget all that, and think about holding that baby. We probably won't get another chance like this one. Your sister loves you. She wants to do something to make you happy."

"I'd have to give up my job at the library."

"The scrapyard, now that Aron's on board, brings enough money in for all four of us." Billy put both arms around her. "Go on, take Ez up on her offer. You know you want to."

"I do want to, but I don't want to. Billy, there's so many potential pitfalls to consider."

Billy chuckled.

"Don't consider. Just do it."

"You're all for it, aren't you?"

"Yeah." Billy yawned. "I suppose I am."

She let silence envelop them until Billy's arms began to relax around her.

"And what about Aron?" Eden added. "Doesn't he have a say in this?"

The only reply was Billy's even breaths and the odd gentle snore.

Eden sighed. *Could she spend the rest of her life childless if she had to?* She closed her eyes and came to the conclusion that yes, she could, but there would be a large hole in her life where a baby should be. Her arms ached to hold a warm, wriggling bundle of joy. There would only be a few more years left before she started to look like a kid's grandmother at the school gates. *Why was life so bloody unfair?*

Chapter Four

Aron Jones felt he had a pretty good insight into his wife's moods. However, this time he knew there was something on her mind, but was certain he had not done anything that would place him in the dog house. She was quieter than usual, and slightly more impatient with the boys. He decided to broach the subject of what he could possibly have done wrong after making sure he had taken his turn at bathing James and Jared and had read them a bedtime story.

With a last warning to his sons to keep the noise down, he sought out Esme, swinging thoughtfully on the canopied garden seat.

"Boys all done. Just waiting for a kiss from their mummy."

"Okay. Thanks. I'll go up."

He sat in her still-warm seat. Presently she returned and flopped down next to him.

"Anything wrong?" Aron swung the seat with one foot.

"No…er…not really."

"Come on, out with it. You've been quiet for days. What've I done this time?"

He was surprised when she snuggled up to him. If he'd managed to piss her off, he knew it would have been time to be given the old freeze job.

"Nothing, it's not you."

He relaxed and gave her a squeeze.

"Who then?"

"Oh, it's Eden. I know she's hurting, and not just with actual pain. I feel for her and the misery of knowing that she'll never be a mother. That is… unless I help."

Aron was intrigued, but puzzled.

"How the hell can you help? There's nothing anyone can do."

"There is." Esme looked up at him. "I can have a baby for her."

Aron collected his thoughts for a moment before replying.

"Not with me, you can't. I'm firing blanks. Anyway, I know you... you'd never be able to give it up."

"I could, for my sister. All Billy needs to do is give me the sperm in a pot. I could do the rest."

"Christ!" Aron replied with some force. "You've got this all worked out, haven't you?"

Esme nodded.

"Yeah, I suppose I have. The boys are at school now, so I can rest during the day at the end of the pregnancy. If we do it now Eden will be a mother by the spring. I feel sure she wants this so much but she's frightened to say yes. "

Birds chirruped in the trees. And the sun still shone. All was normal, but Aron felt his life was about to undergo a massive upheaval, and not necessarily for the better.

"I'm not happy about it, but I can't stop you. I know you won't rest until you do this for your sister, but hey, it's *your* body. All I can say is that it'll probably end in tears."

"Thank you." Esme kissed his cheek. "There will be no problems, I can assure you. She turned me down the first time, but I'm going to ask her again. If all four of us are present, she might change her mind.

***

Aron felt decidedly uncomfortable. He took a swig of cold beer and glanced at the smiling faces of Eden and Billy depicted on the wall above their mantelpiece and then turned back to reality. He could tell that Billy was happy enough with the suggestion, but Eden's expression gave away more than she let on.

"Ez, we already talked about this."

Aron felt Eden's attention shift to him.

"Aron, what do you think?"

"It's up to Ez." Aron replied with a shrug. "She's got her mind set on it."

"But your wife will be carrying another man's child!" Eden ran a hand distractedly through her hair. "And what about your boys? They'll know there's a baby on the way. How will they cope when Ez gives it up?"

"Kids are adaptable. At least they'll get to see their half-sister or brother regularly."

Aron hoped he had said the right thing. He looked at his brother-in-law.

"How about you, Bill?" What do you think about it?"

Billy finished the last of his beer before speaking.

"I think it'd be great to have a nipper running around. It's what we've always wanted, but Eden's worried that Ez will become too attached to it. I think that's the main problem."

"I'll be its auntie, but that's all." Esme replied. "Come on Ede, you know you want a baby. I can give you one. We can even draw up a contract if you like, although when I looked online into making a surrogacy agreement I found out it wouldn't be enforceable by UK law."

"There's nothing I'd like more than to hold my own baby." Eden replied. "You know that already. Hey…you're my sister. You've never let me down before. But it's such a big ask of someone."

"Get over it. I'm doing it." Esme raised her right thumb. "Okay?"

There was a few seconds' silence before Eden spoke.

"Okay. But..."

"No *buts*. It's done and dusted. Do you trust me? Do you want to discuss a surrogacy agreement? Unfortunately here in the UK Aron and I will be the baby's legal parents, but we can change that with a court order after the birth, but it might take a while to do.

Eden shook her head.

"If an agreement isn't enforceable by law, then what's the point of having one? More importantly I trust my own sister. We don't need to go through all the pseudo-legal stuff."

"Let's celebrate!" Esme stood up. "Aron, have we still got that champagne left over from Christmas?"

Aron nodded.

"Sure. I'll go and get it."

He was pleased to be out of the room for a moment. He switched on the cellar light, took a deep breath in, climbed down the steps and enjoyed the brief silence. He could partly share in Eden's misgivings when he casted his mind back eight years to when the boys were born and Esme's almost feral protection of them, but was certain his wife would never do anything to make her sister even more miserable than she already was. Anyway, Billy was up for it. Aron took a bottle of Dom Perignon 2001 from the holder, climbed back up the stairs, and switched off the light.

Chapter Five

Billy Reece unlocked the scrapyard gate and grinned to himself at the thought of possibly being a father the following year. In the distance he could hear the engine of his brother-in-law's motorbike as it broke the silence of the sultry morning.

Aron rode up to the yard, revved the bike and then turned off the ignition.

"Noisy bastard. You've frightened the birds!"

Aron gave Billy the middle finger.

"What birds?" He took off his crash helmet and looked about. "Who have you got tucked away in the office?"

"Julia Roberts."

"She's getting on a bit now, isn't she?"

Billy laughed and took the padlock from the main door of a ramshackle-looking caravan, which served as their office. Aron walked to his desk and divested himself of his rucksack and heavy Kevlar clothing. Billy switched the kettle on.

"So… you're going to impregnate my wife?"

"From a distance." Billy nodded. "I'm looking forward to it."

"You do the best bit, then I get the morning sickness, aches and pains and piles?"

Billy rinsed two grimy cups under the cold tap, then added a spoonful of coffee to each and then hot water when the kettle boiled.

"You should take more bran with it, mate."

He proffered a steaming cup to Aron.

"And no, I won't need that stash of porno mags under your bed either."

Aron grinned and then looked out of the window.

"Looks like old Jim's back for the wing mirror off that Merc."

"He's early." Billy took a sip of coffee. "I'll go. You just sit on your arse."

Aron gazed idly at his brother-in-law talking to the first customer of the day. He still wasn't sure how he felt regarding the whole situation, but now the deed would soon be done and his wife would actually be pregnant with Billy's child. A sinking feeling settled in his stomach, and he rued the day he had bragged to his drinking buddies about how easy it had been to undergo a vasectomy.

A large breakdown van and trailer motored slowly in through the yard gates complete with a badly damaged Honda Civic. Aron finished his coffee and went outside. Even at 09:30 the sun was merciless.

***

It had been a busy morning and they were both hungry by 11:30. Aron inspected the inside of his sandwich.

"Bloody hell. Cheese again."

Billy opened his lunch box and grimaced.

"I hate tuna and sweetcorn. I can smell it from here. I'll swap if you like?"

"Yeah." Aron slid his sandwich along the table with a grimy hand. "Er... how will it work then? You know... the actual...er..."

"I'm an expert, mate. We've had years of practise. Ez will have to be at the right moment in her monthlies, round about two weeks after a period starts for most women. Eden used to take her temperature every morning, but she was six weeks coming on and six weeks going off."

Aron grinned.

"Why the thermometer? I only had to look at Ez and she was pregnant."

"Ovulation, you wanker." Billy chewed as he spoke. "Her temperature will be higher when she ovulates."

Aron swallowed.

"Er… where will she need to put the thermometer?"

Billy roared with laughter.

"Where do you think? Under her tongue! Christ, mate, you don't know a lot, do you?"

"Not really." Aron shrugged. "I know how to strip and engine down though."

"Well, that won't do you much good when it comes to getting Ez pregnant, will it?"

"I'm not the one that'll be getting her up the duff." Aron replied. "That's your job."

Billy rolled his eyes.

"But *you're* the one who'll be in bed with her in the mornings. Get her to take her temperature first thing, and then let me know real quick when it goes up."

"Yeah, just as long as nothing else goes up."

"Straight." Billy took another bite. "Don't worry. It'll be a test tube jobby."

"What do you think Barry and Janet will say?" Aron looked questioningly at Billy.

"Let the girls speak to them." Billy waved away his question with one sweep of his hand. "We're only the sons-in-law. We don't count."

Chapter Six

A clock ticked loudly in the silence. Janet Prentice tried not to let her mouth hang open in surprise.

"Are you sure this is want you want?"

"Of course, Mum" Esme nodded. "We've all discussed it."

"So why are you here?"

"To let you know of course." Eden replied. "Before things all kick off. I'm feeling a bit better now, and Ez is going to try a first go next week."

Barry Prentice coughed gently.

"So long as the four of you are happy with it, then it's got nothing to do with us."

Esme regarded her father with a puzzled expression.

"Dad, it's got *everything* to do with you. You'll be getting a new grandchild hopefully."

Barry gave a smile that did not quite reach his eyes.

"And what does Billy and Aron's parents have to say?"

"We haven't told them yet." Eden replied. "We're going to do that next. In fact, I think we ought to go and do it now, before the boys get home from the yard. I'll phone Pamela and Donna, and tell them to come to my house. It might sound better coming straight from us."

She stood up, still somewhat stiffly, and looked at Esme.

"Shall we go?"

***

They stood in the doorway and watched Esme drive away. Janet returned Eden's wave from the passenger window. Barry shook his head slowly.

"I don't like the sound of it. It won't work."

"Let them get on with it." Janet closed the door behind them. "You're right. It hasn't got anything to do with us."

Barry nodded.

"Ez will hold that baby in her arms, and that will be that."

"You know it and I know it." Janet replied. "But Eden doesn't. It'll break her heart."

Barry nodded.

"And we'll have to pick up the pieces. What a mess it'll be."

They walked along the hallway towards the back door that led into the garden. Janet picked up a watering can.

"Especially if Billy fights for custody."

Barry began to hoe along the nearest flowerbed with more than his usual force."

"I think I want to move to Spain."

Janet laughed.

"We need to be here for Eden. Apart from Billy, we're all she's got. Fat lot of good we'll be in Spain."

"Shall I have a quiet word with Billy?" Barry looked up from weeding. "Perhaps I can make him see sense."

"Janet shook her head.

"Don't interfere between husband and wife. They won't thank you for it."

Barry thrust the hoe into the ground.

"But I don't want to stand by and see Eden even more upset! She's been through so much over the past few years. She has to accept it's just nature's way. Some women will never become mothers - not every woman has that right."

"I know." Janet agreed with a nod. "But you can't tell a woman *that* who is desperate for a child. She'll move heaven and hell to get what she wants."

Barry pulled up some convolvulus vine.

"You *can't* always get what you want. Even Mick Jagger and Keith Richards wrote a song about it. Acceptance is the key here."

"Yeah, but you know she'll never accept it." Janet put down the watering can and sat on a nearby bench. "It's a shame we have to stay schtum, but hey, that's what we have to do now that our kids are grown. If only I could have a word with Billy…"

"Why do women always want babies?" Barry grumbled and sat down beside her. "Us men have to work our arses off to keep them."

"Ah, but they bring you joy, don't they?" Janet smiled. "And *us girls* only have a small window to procreate. It's all right for you men, but by the time we get to thirty five our biological clock is ticking away the hours. Eden's thirty six, bless her. Being a mother is all she's ever wanted."

Barry sighed.

"They need to adopt. It might work out better for them."

"That could take years, and might cost them thousands to achieve their goal. It's usually older children who are waiting to be adopted, and Eden wants a baby. It's difficult trying to foist your values and morals on an older child whose guardians might have had totally different views. Some adopted kids tend to be a bit confused, feel unloved, and therefore are a bit of a handful."

"Oh gawd." Barry chuckled. "Not good then."

Chapter Seven

Eden kept up a smiling countenance as Pamela Reece and Donna Jones regarded her with open mouths.

"You're having me on, aren't you?" Pamela shook her head. "Please tell me you're joking!"

"I'm perfectly serious." Eden looked at Esme for support. "Esme and Aron already have their family. Ez wants to do this for me out of the goodness of her heart, as now of course without her help I'll never become a mother."

"It's absolutely true." Esme nodded. "I don't see what all the fuss is about."

Donna walked over to her daughter-in-law and gave her a hug.

"Ez, I think it's great what you're planning to do. It took Steve and me months to conceive, and I still remember the total desolation every time another period started."

Eden felt buoyed by Donna's remark.

"Thanks Donna. I didn't know you'd had problems too."

Donna shrugged.

"Oh, years ago now of course. I was lucky to have Aron. We tried for another child for years, but nothing ever happened. By then we felt too old to adopt."

"Well, I assume the four of you know what you're doing." Pamela sniffed. "Will my son be the biological father?"

"Yes." Eden replied. "Absolutely."

She took the subsequent silence to interpret the older women's unspoken thoughts.

"And don't worry, there'll be no funny business."

Esme laughed.

"What she means is that Billy and I won't be having sex."

Eden suppressed a giggle and was surprised to see her mother-in-law blush.

"Thank goodness. I brought my son up with morals."

"So did I." Donna nodded. "I like the idea, but I can't see Aron going for this. What a cock up."

Eden roared with laughter.

"Exactly! Billy will rise manfully to the occasion and do his bit, I'm sure."

Pamela momentarily covered her burning face with one hand.

"Oh goodness, do I really need to hear all the ins and outs of this?"

"There's a joke there somewhere." Eden giggled again. "We just thought it would be polite to tell you what's going on. You're going to be a granny soon, Pam."

"Lovely…I think, and it's a shame Billy's dad isn't alive to see his future grandchild. Pamela exhaled slowly. "I have misgivings, but hey, it's not really up to me is it?"

***

Eden waved to Donna in the passenger seat as Pamela drove away, and then walked back with Esme towards the house.

"I'm sure Pam thinks we're crazy."

"Who cares what either of them think?" Esme chuckled. "Donna will tell Steve and I bet he'll try to talk Aron out of it, but I'm going to have a baby for you, and that's all there is to it."

Eden felt a shiver of excitement.

"I can hardly believe it. After all these years Billy and I are going to be parents!"

"Get used to it, Sis." Esme nudged Eden in the ribs. "'Cos it's going to happen."

Eden drew an excited breath.

"I don't know how I can ever thank you."

"You won't thank me at two o'clock in the morning when you've been woken up *yet again* by a screaming baby." Esme laughed. "We had a double whammy of course. Some nights we just took turns in sleeping because at least then we knew we'd get *some* sleep. But hey, those times soon pass and you end up with a little human being, or in our case *two*, who eats what you give him and sleeps at the same time that you do."

"Can't wait." Eden grinned. "I just *know* that my baby will sleep all night and never scream!"

"I wouldn't bank on that." Esme shook her head. "Take it from one who's been there, done that, and got the sick-stained tee shirt."

Chapter Eight

It was all down to *him* now. Ez's temperature had gone up, and the pressure was intense. Billy, naked after a shower, opened a porn magazine, looked at the genitals on display, and felt about as aroused as a cold suet pudding.

"How are you getting on in there?"

His wife standing outside the bathroom door and hopping from foot to foot did not help matters.

"Er...I'll let you know."

He turned a page to scenes of cunnilingus that would make a schoolboy blush, but at the same moment remembered a voicemail from Manchetts.

"I've got to phone Aron. Manchetts are bringing two Fiestas to the yard about five thirty. He needs to hang on."

"I'll tell him." Eden's muffled voice answered in an instant. "You carry on in there."

Her footsteps receded. Billy sighed and turned another page. A well-endowed blonde in a basque and not much else invited him into her parlour. Billy was hungry and decided he'd rather have a hot dinner. He threw on a dressing gown, put the sample pot and magazine under his arm, and went out onto the landing. Eden's voice echoed up the stairs.

"All done?"

"No." Billy replied. "I need some help. Did you talk to Aron."

Eden appeared at the foot of the stairwell.

"Yeah, he knows. What do you mean about needing help?"

He winked at her from the upstairs landing.

"Porno mags don't do it for me. I need the real thing."

Her features remained impassive.

"It's not been six weeks yet. I feel about as sexy as a wet Wednesday in Wakefield."

"Why Wakefield?" Billy laughed. "What happens on a Wednesday?"

"Absolutely nothing, especially in the afternoons." Eden grinned at him as she climbed back up. "Come on, you've got to make an effort. Ez will only be fertile for about two days, you know that."

"Well, get your kit off then, come and lay down with me, and we'll see what comes up."

"Okay, I'll give it a go, but there's a big scar where there wasn't one before. It ain't pretty."

"I don't care." Billy came forward and gave her a kiss. "I love you. It makes no difference to me. Come and give us a hand, so to speak."

***

"Thank Christ for that!"

Billy flopped back on the pillows and wiped his sweaty brow with one hand. Eden twisted the lid closed on a pot of creamy liquid, leapt up from the bed and threw on her clothes.

"Come on, you've got to drive me over to Ez's. I'm not allowed to drive for another two weeks." She pushed the pot into her bra. "I'm going to keep it warm in *here*."

"Lucky old pot." Billy yawned. "I just need to lie here for a minute."

Eden pulled at his flaccid member.

"No time. Hurry!"

Billy removed his wife's hand and reluctantly stood up.

"Is that it? Am I redundant now?"

"No." Eden threw a pair of pants and trousers in his direction. "You'll have to keep the baby fed and watered for the next twenty years."

"Can't I have a cup of tea first?"

"No!"

Grumbling slightly, Billy finished dressing and followed Eden outside. She climbed carefully into the passenger seat.

"Put your clog on it. These sperms are swimming around with no egg to fertilise. They'll get cheesed off and die."

Billy started the engine and pulled away from the kerb.

"Yeah, I know how they feel. There was I lying naked in bed with my good wife, and now she's more concerned with what's in her bra."

"Stop complaining." Eden replied good-naturedly. "You know you want a baby as much as I do. I'll text Ez and let her know we're on our way."

"I thought I might have had a bit more fun making one first."

"'Fraid not. Time is of the essence."

In ten minutes Billy had pulled up on Esme and Aron's driveway. The front door opened immediately, and Eden climbed out of the passenger seat and gingerly handed over the pot to Esme before getting back into the car.

"Job done. We can go home now."

"Aren't we going to be offered tea and biscuits? I'm knackered!"

"You can have your afters when we get back." Eden grinned.

Billy squeezed her knee.

"I'll hold you to that. Come to think of it, Ez had better get on with it, so perhaps it's best we're not around."

"Just imagine…" Eden looked at him. "Our child could be conceived tonight."

"Yeah."

They rode in silence for a while, until Billy took a detour. Eden looked out of the window.

"Where are you going?"

"Oh, I need to stop at the yard. I want a word with the chap from Manchetts."

Chapter Nine

Aron tried to concentrate on the TV programme, but his mind kept registering the fact that Esme might now be carrying another man's baby. A recent conversation with his father had cast much gloom on his decision to go ahead. He dismissed a fleeting pang of envy that he could no longer impregnate his wife, and took a sideways glance at her from his armchair. Her expression resembled the cat who had not only got the cream, but also the bowl of salmon as well.

"Did you…?"

"Yeah, I've done it. Billy, and Eden so don't worry, came round earlier on. That's why he took the day off."

Aron nodded.

"Yeah, he told me. So now we wait?"

"We wait." Esme agreed. "I'll either get a period, or I won't. It's all in the lap of the gods."

The advert break came on the screen. Aron muted the sound and looked at his wife.

"Do you wish we'd had more children?"

"No." Esme shook her head. "I've got my hands full enough every day looking after the boys. Have you changed your mind then?"

"Not really… I just wondered, that's all."

Esme put her feet up on the coffee table and leaned back in her chair.

"That's okay then. I don't want you getting broody and sloping off to have your vasectomy reversed without telling me."

Aron grinned.

"Is that the equivalent of you girls stopping the pill and not letting on?"

Esme grinned at Aron.

"Touché."

"How did you er… do it? What did you use?"

Esme, eyes on the screen for the return of the programme, answered distractedly.

"That old syringe that we used to pour Calpol down the boys' throats with. I found it in the medicine cupboard. I washed it and rinsed it out thoroughly and it worked a treat."

"Oh."

So that was all there was to it; no loving caresses between a man and a woman. Aron already felt sorry for the baby, that it had not been conceived through love. An old syringe could not compare to the undulating waves of pleasure that bonded husband and wife together in the act of procreation. He recalled the romantic holiday in Venice over eight years previously that resulted in the birth of their sons. He watched the TV programme with unseeing eyes, all the while wishing the sperm inside his wife was that of his own.

***

He could not help but feel relief when her morning sickness failed to materialise. When Esme complained that she felt period pains returning, he remained tactfully silent but still offered his usual comforting presence. Three days' later at the first sight of blood, her tears began and she sobbed on his shoulder.

"You'll have to tell Billy this morning, when you get to work. I'll phone Eden and let her know."

"There'll be plenty more opportunities." Aron gave her a hug. "Yeah, I'll tell Billy. Sometimes it takes months, you know that."

"Yeah, yeah." Esme sniffed. "But I got pregnant straight away with the twins. I thought it would be like that again."

Aron kissed the top of her head.

"That was a while ago now. Perhaps it's because you're older."

He regretted his remark straight away, as it brought forth a fresh wave of tears.

"You really know what to say to a girl, don't you! Thirty-one isn't that old!"

Aron remembered how Billy had told him that women over 30 were considered 'elderly' in the medical profession when it came to conceiving babies. However, he decided that he had said enough. He gave his wife one last squeeze, and wiped her eyes with his fingers.

"Got to hurry off to work now, but go and see Eden. There might not be so much time soon, as the boys will break up next week for the summer."

"Okay."

He grabbed his car keys and lunch box, and with a strangely light heart walked out the door towards his van.

***

"'Morning Bill." Aron raised one arm as he strode through the office door.

"Hey there."

Billy looked keenly at him, trying to read his expression. Aron decided to get it over with straight away.

"Sorry, mate. Her monthlies started this morning, but plenty more goes yet, eh?"

He knew his brother-in-law inside out; Billy would not show one iota that he cared one way or the other.

"Sure, absolutely."

The phone rang, and Aron, relieved, grabbed the receiver.

"Reece and Jones."

"Aron, it's Dad."

"Oh, hi."

"I just wanted to find out how it's going... you know, with Ez getting pregnant. Mum told me."

"Er... no joy."

"I wanted to speak to you when Ez wasn't around. I'll say this again... knock it on the head, son."

Aron glanced at Billy and sighed.

"Can't, I'm afraid."

"Then don't say I didn't warn you."

"Okay."

The line went dead. Aron put the phone down.

"Who was that?" Billy looked up. "Was that Stan Bradley?"

Aron shook his head.

"No, someone who wanted a catalytic converter for an X Type Jag."

"We haven't got one in at the moment."

"That's what I told him."

Chapter Ten

With a heavy heart Esme rang the bell with tears still running down her face.

"Hey! What are you doing here?"

Esme could not speak. Her sister's expression changed from surprise to despair within seconds. They hugged on the doorstep.

"So sorry, Ede. We'll try again next month, yeah?"

Eden turned away, sobbing. Esme closed the door, followed Eden into the front room, and sat down beside her on the sofa.

"I'm only thirty one. There's loads more time yet."

Eden sighed.

"For you, yeah, but not for the eggs. Don't you think I know that? Don't you think I know everything there is to know about the female reproductive system?"

"I'll try again, again and again, and then I'll try one more time. Billy will get sick of producing sperm."

She was glad to see a little spark of a smile to cross her sister's face.

"He's got the best bit, hasn't he?"

"It would appear so." Esme nodded. "Has he ever had it tested?"

"Tested?" Eden looked thoughtful. "Maybe, I don't remember. The fault is with *me* though, not him."

"Better make sure all those little sammies are up to the job." Esme replied. "It might have been his fault all along."

Eden sniffed and shook her head.

"No. I'm sure he would have been tested at the clinic. Jeez, we had enough doctors prodding and poking about. They would have spotted something wrong there, for sure."

She hated to see Eden so depressed. Esme put her arm around her sister and gave her a squeeze.

"Come on, I'm taking you out shopping for a little bit of retail therapy. We're going to buy some baby clothes, because I *know* they'll be needed one day."

"Oh, no." Eden shook her head. "I couldn't possibly."

"Yeah, you can. I won't take no for an answer. We've got until half past two, and then I have to go and pick the boys up from school. So grab your bag and let's get going."

She took a moment to compose herself whilst Eden got ready. Esme wiped her eyes with a tissue, blew her nose, and checked her make-up in a small hand mirror. When her sister returned, she felt more like her old self.

"Ready?"

"O…kay." Eden sounded unconvinced. "But I want to leave it another week before I drive anywhere."

Esme made her way to the front door.

"That's fine, I'll do the honours. Let's rock!

***

The welcome air-conditioned coolness of the shopping mall was balm to her soul. Esme steered Eden away from the sight of a pregnant woman wearing a flowery sundress who pushed a smiling toddler in a buggy along as she window-shopped, and guided her towards an indoor clothes market. The stall holders looked at them expectantly as they passed by. Esme pointed to the last stall in the row.

"That's where I used to buy the boys' clothes from. He's still there… come on."

Eden pulled back.

"I'm not going to buy anything. It's bad luck."

Esme took hold of her sister's arm.

"Listen…you've had more than your share of bad luck. It's time for nice things to happen to you. Okay, so you're superstitious, but I'm going to buy something adorable for my future niece or nephew, so bear with me."

She enjoyed inspecting the romper suits, matinee coats and bootees laid out on the stall. She picked out a white Babygro, a colourful bib and pair of white bootees, and a tiny pale yellow cardigan knitted lovingly by hand. As she was handed her purchases, Esme turned and gave them to Eden.

"I want to see my niece or nephew wearing these, so keep hold of them."

"Yes *ma'am*." Eden laughed and made a mock salute. "I could kill for a cup of coffee though."

***

Esme's heart sank at the proliferation of pre-school children in the café. Everywhere there were babies crying, toddlers in highchairs, and three year olds running about. She looked at Eden.

"Do you want to go somewhere else?"

"No, it's okay." Eden shook her head. "The world is full of pregnant ladies and children that aren't mine. I can't hide away forever from that fact."

Esme nodded. "My round. It was my idea to come shopping. What do you want?"

"Just a coffee."

Balancing two coffees on a tray, she looked around for Eden, who had found a table in the furthest corner of the café and sat facing the wall as she wrote a text.

"Here you go." She placed the cups down. "Billy?"

Eden nodded.

"Yeah, Aron's obviously told him the good news."

"Don't worry. It'll work next time. I *know* it will. It's got to… I've bought the Babygro now."

***

"We've got to go through all that again in another couple of weeks?"

Esme nodded to Aron as she supervised the boys attempting to eat spaghetti Bolognese without spilling it on their clothes.

"Yep. She doesn't let on, but Eden's ready to crack, I think. I have to do this for her. I have to keep an eye out for ovulation."

"Who's ov-u-lation? Jared sucked up a mouthful of spaghetti.

Esme suppressed a grin.

"Not *who*… *what*. You don't need to be bothered with that for a few years yet."

James gave Jared a nudge.

"It's a monster who hides under your bed. He chops off your willie in the night."

"No…*your* willie." Jared stuck out his tongue at his brother.

Esme glared at her sons. Aron, bringing a forkful of Bolognese to his lips, spluttered with laughter.

"Will you two stop talking about willies at the table!"

"Sorry Mum".

Two pairs of identical grey eyes regarded her seriously. Esme bit her lip and made the mistake of turning to Aron, who exploded with laughter. Esme erupted in giggles, closely followed by the twins.

"There's too many willies around here." Esme laughed. "What a bloody family!"

"Willies are best." James grinned. "We don't want any sisters."

"And you won't be having any either."

Jared sucked up a long strand of spaghetti.

"Can we have some brothers then?"

"*Some* brothers?" Esme chuckled. "How many do you want?"

"Two."

Esme shook her head.

"I don't think so. Eat your dinner."

"Oh...." Both boys whined in unison. "We want a brother..."

"Well, you're not getting one."

Aron's abrupt tone had put paid to the moment of jollity. Esme wondered how her sons might possibly cope with a little brother that she would have to give away.

Chapter Eleven

After three failed insemination attempts, Billy had had enough. He packed up his fishing gear on a still-hot Sunday morning in October, whilst Eden slept. He left a note on her dressing table, knowing full well another call from Esme was probably due that day, and before the whole euphoric/depressive cycle would begin all over again.

'Gone fishing. Need a break from being a stud bull. Be back tonight, and no, I didn't leave any maggots in the fridge. See you later. xxx'

The production of sperm to order had begun to grate on his nerves. He crept out the front door and clicked it quietly shut. He hoped the double glazing would be enough to mask the sound of the van's rattle, and felt a lightening of his mood as he pointed his car in the direction of Needham Lake.

Only one other fisherman had beaten him to it; Len. Billy, laden with a bag of gear, gave Len a nod of acknowledgement as he walked past towards his official jetty under a tree alongside the path parallel to the railway line that ran along the other side of a high brick wall.

Only a family of swans and their cygnets were about that early in the morning to disturb the glass-like stillness of the water. Billy put down his bag, turned off his phone, and settled down into a fold-up canvas chair to unpack the gear.

It was too soon for the general public to be about. A lone jogger's footsteps could be heard on the path behind him, and there was a gentle breeze blowing in his face. Billy drew a deep breath and reflected as he drank in the quietness of the morning and set up his tripod stand.

Was his sperm defective in some way? *How come two women now had failed to get pregnant?* *Had he been at fault the whole bloody time?* He extended out his fishing rod and attached the reel as Len expertly pulled a bream from the murky waters of the lake.

The whole baby thing now was getting on his tits. Billy fed a line through the hoops along the rod, and attached the float, hook and bait. He needed to postpone a fourth cycle of listening to Eden crying all night.

He cast out with possibly more force than was necessary, and watched the float as it bobbed mesmerisingly upon the water. He pulled out the little camping gas stove from his kit, and set a one-cup kettle to boil with water from a container.

There was nobody to bother him, and he cared not two hoots whether he caught a fish or not. Demands on him were few on days like these, and other fishermen tended to keep to themselves. Billy relaxed a little, put on his baseball cap, and raised his closed eyes to the sun.

"I thought I'd find you by the lake."

Billy sighed with irritation at the familiar voice and looked over his right shoulder. Aron stood on the jetty complete with a six pack of IPA. His first thought was to tell his brother-in-law to fuck off, but decided in the interest of family relations it was better to hold that remark.

"What the hell are you doing here?"

"The girls have been trying to get in touch with you. I've been given instructions to bring you back dead or alive. Ez's temperature went up this morning."

The kettle came to the boil. Billy added a spoonful of coffee to an enamel mug and poured on the hot water.

"I've only got one cup."

"That's all right." Aron held up the six-pack. "I'll have a beer. There's more for you here if you like."

"Cheers. I don't drink beer if I'm fishing."

Aron squatted down beside him and took a swig out of the can.

"Everything all right, mate?"

"No, not really." Billy replied. "Everything's shite."

"Just one more try, eh?" Aron looked up at him. "If it doesn't work this time, we'll have a couple of months off and try again after Christmas. What d'you say?"

"I say this… is there anybody who wants me for something other than what's in my balls?"

Aron chuckled.

"Yeah, we all do, mate, but your balls are the most important thing at the moment. There's liquid gold in there. It's all right for you, but I might as well be a eunuch."

The float bobbed about, and Billy reeled in his first catch of the day, a good sized perch.

"It's at least seven inches."

"Yeah, you wish." Aron stood up. "Bring your balls home. They're not much good to man nor beast out here."

"They're having a rest." Billy unhooked the perch and put it back in the lake. "Men and beasts don't do it for me."

Aron gave Billy's back a playful slap.

"Come back and do your bit, eh?"

"Later on." Billy mumbled. "Just let me sit here for a while first. It's a bloody peaceful way to spend a Sunday."

"Yeah?" Aron replied with interest. "If you say so."

Chapter Twelve

She lay supine on the bed, with her legs raised on three feather pillows. Aron had dutifully played his part and taken the twins out for a train ride to Trafalgar Square to feed the pigeons, and she was alone for the first time in ages. As the stillness of the house settled all around her, Esme closed her eyes and willed Billy's sperm to find their goal.

Work this time, you little bastards!

In her mind she went deep inside her body, to where millions of life-giving sperm raced for first prize. She singled out the biggest and fastest spermatozoa and willed it along to a glowing egg at one end of her fallopian tube. Then she prayed to God, smiled, and fell into a light doze.

***

She knew she was pregnant as soon as even a week and a half had gone by. Her breasts were sore, and her period, usually like clockwork, had failed to arrive. Esme felt faintly nauseous but excited all at the same time. She hugged herself and jumped up and down in the privacy of their en-suite bathroom.

She heard Aron's light tap on the door.

"You all right in there?"

"Yeah, great." Esme replied. "I think it's worked."

She came out freshly showered and wrapped in a towel, and nearly bumped into Aron standing by the door.

"You're pregnant?"

Esme noticed the fact that he was unsmiling.

49

"I'm sure I am." She replied. "You can give the good news to Billy when you get to the yard, and I'll go and see Ede." She hesitated, then shook her head. "No, actually, I'd better get a test done first. I'll nip down to the supermarket and get one of those Clear Blue things."

She moved towards the wardrobe, but then turned mid-way and looked over her shoulder.

"You don't seem very pleased."

Aron shrugged.

"Sure, I'm pleased for Eden." He replied in as upbeat a tone as he could manage. "It's great news for them."

"I've even worked out when I'll be due – July the twenty seventh."

Aron nodded.

"But best to confirm it first, eh?

Esme threw on some underwear, jeans and a short sleeved top.

"Sure, but I *feel* different, just like I did before. I'll do the test first thing tomorrow morning. I've already been to the loo now."

She bustled contentedly about in the kitchen making coffee and toast for herself, and bacon rolls for Aron. However, she was unhappy with her husband's response; by now they should both have been dancing about the room with joy, but his reply to her news was lukewarm to say the least.

***

She was up bright and early at 05:50, half an hour before the alarm. Leaving Aron asleep, Esme climbed carefully out of bed and crept into the en-suite. The Clear Blue testing kit sat atop the medicine cabinet, and Esme took it out of the box and re-read the instructions once again just to make sure.

The test was easy enough to carry out, and the resulting bold blue line on the display caused an involuntary scream to erupt from her throat. At once the bathroom door flew open, startling her.

"What the fuck's the matter?" Aron, half asleep, rubbed his eyes."

"Look!" Esme shoved the display screen in front of his eyes. "I'm pregnant!"

"Congratulations."

Aron moved past her to the sink and splashed cold water on his face. Esme, slightly deflated, checked the blue line again.

"Eden will be pleased, anyway. I'm going to make some tea."

There was no response apart from the noise of the electric shaver. She hid her annoyance and padded downstairs to the kitchen and opened the blind. The colder-than-average night had caused a dew to settle on the grass. Winter was just around the corner, and the long haul to July stretched out endlessly in front of her.

She had coffee and toast ready by the time Aron, in working overalls, entered the kitchen.

"I made your lunchbox up last night. It's in the fridge."

"Cheers." Aron sat down heavily on a chair. "So... you'll make an appointment to see the doc?"

"Yes, I'll get the ball rolling this morning, after I've seen Eden."

He took a sip of coffee.

"Will you tell the boys, or shall I?"

"No problem, I'll do it." Esme replied. "I'll have a think about the best way to word it. They'll need to know that we won't be keeping the baby."

Aron nodded.

"Good luck with that."

"Have you got a problem with the fact that I'm pregnant?"

"No problem." Aron stood up and took his lunch from the fridge. "See you later. I'm going to be late for work."

She looked at the clock. Aron usually left at seven thirty, and it was still only seven o'clock. Esme came to the conclusion that whatever was bothering her husband, he would have to come to terms with it by himself.

"Yeah, see you." Her smile did not quite reach her eyes. "Have a nice day."

His last four words rubbed off any gilt edging to a virtual certificate of pregnancy. It was time to come down to earth. The boys needed breakfast and packed lunches for school. The pile of washing needed sorting into lights and darks, and she needed to check Jared's hair for nits. Esme gave a wry grin as she stepped into the shower; life went on despite the fact that she was now definitely pregnant at last with her sister's baby.

Chapter Thirteen

She could not keep a grin from spreading as soon as the front door opened.

"Guess what?" Esme pointed to her abdomen with one finger.

"Tell me you're not joking!" Eden glanced downwards, her mouth open.

Esme gave her a hug.

"I'm not joking. Got a blue line this morning!"

Eden's face crumpled. Esme hurried inside, and out of sight behind the closed door she held Eden until her shoulders ceased shaking with sobs. It was a full ten minutes before either of them spoke. Eden came out of her sister's embrace and wiped her eyes with the backs of her hands.

"Oh God, you don't know how long I've waited for this!" Eden drew in a shaky breath. "Thank you *so* much!"

Esme wiped her own eyes with a tissue.

"It makes me happy to be able to do it for you. Aron was going to tell Billy this morning."

"At least he or she will have one outfit to wear!" Eden replied with a trace of a smile. "Come on, I'll put the kettle on to celebrate."

"There's plenty of time to buy a whole wardrobe full."

Esme followed behind and perched herself upon one of the high stools at the breakfast bar. Eden's posture seemed somehow more upright already, and she was pleased to hear her sister quietly humming to herself as she bustled around making tea. She opened one of the cupboards and took out a packet of chocolate biscuits.

"I shall open these to celebrate. You're eating for two now."

"Steady on!" Esme laughed. "I'll be Two Ton Tessie before too long if I start on those."

She took one biscuit out of politeness.

"I'm going to make an appointment at the doctor's surgery today. You can come with me to all my ante-natal appointments if you like, but if the boys are off school through holidays or sickness you might have to look after *them* instead?"

"Oh yes, that won't be a problem, I'd love to on both counts. I think I'll give three months' notice at the library in April, and then I'll be around to help you in the later stages." Eden nodded. "Thank you a thousand times. You're going to make me a mother, and I'm so happy. I don't know what else to say."

Esme laughed.

"You don't have to say anything. But I want to say something…"

"What?" Eden looked at her with interest.

"Where's that bloody cup of tea?"

***

The GP regarded Esme over his reading glasses.

"Yes, from the examination I can confirm that you are in the early stage of pregnancy. Living in Newmarket as you do, you can have a choice of which hospital you'd like to attend for your ante-natal appointments and the birth. You can either go to the Rosie at Cambridge, or to the West Suffolk at Bury Saint Edmunds."

It was on the tip of her tongue to reply, but at the last moment she turned to Eden.

"Any preference?"

"Oh no." Eden shook her head. "Whatever you want."

"Well, the boys were born at Ipswich Hospital, but we've moved since then. I think we'll try the West Suffolk as we've had out-patient appointments there and I hate the Cambridge traffic."

"I shall get the ball rolling with all the paperwork." The GP tapped into his computer. "Obs and Gynae at Bury will look after you very well. You'll get your first appointment through the post. Going on the date of your last period, your due date would be around the twenty seventh of July next year, but a scan around twelve weeks will confirm that."

"Yes." Esme nodded. "I thought it was around then too."

She stood up, closely followed by Eden.

"Thanks, Doctor."

"My pleasure."

***

She ushered the boys to the table when she heard Aron's motor bike outside, and dished up their favourite fillet steak meal with mushrooms, beef tomatoes, chips and peas. The pregnancy had caused her to acquire a strange aversion to meat, and Esme had prepared herself a cheese salad instead.

"Wow, chips!" Jared looked at his plate approvingly. "We hardly ever have chips!"

"Or meat!" James grinned and applied himself to the task of eating.

Esme gave them a wink.

"Make the most of it, because I don't think it's going to last. Now be good the pair of you, and tuck in. I'll just go and say hello to Dad."

She smoothed down her hair and was at the door to greet him as he turned off the bike's engine. She smiled at him.

"Hi."

Aron took off his crash helmet and unbuttoned the top of his jacket.

"All right?"

"How did it go telling Billy?"

He moved past her into the hallway.

"He's as happy as a pig in shit."

"Dinner's ready." Esme felt vaguely uneasy. "The boys are already up the table."

"I'll be there in a minute."

She returned to the kitchen, sat down and looked at her salad. Her appetite had vanished.

"Hello Dad!" James shouted. "Dinner's ready!"

Jared, with his mouth full of chips, waved his fork about.

"Hurry up, Dad! It's getting cold!"

She looked up as Aron appeared in the doorway. Unsmiling, he took his place at the table and began eating mechanically. Esme pushed some cous cous around her plate before making her announcement.

"Boys, I've got something to tell you."

Two small blond heads turned in her direction. Aron cut up his steak with seemingly unnecessary force.

"Mummy's going to have another baby, but it's not ours to keep. Aunty Ede cannot have children, and so when Mummy has this baby she's going to give it to Aunty Ede."

Jared stopped chewing while he digested the information. She thought James' expression showed signs of disappointment.

"But it'll be *our* baby." Jared speared another chip on his fork. "You can't give it away."

"No, you can't give it away." James repeated.

Esme thought for a second before replying.

"It won't be fair for us to have three children and Aunty Ede none, will it?

The twins, now quieter than usual, shook their heads in unison. Aron, silent, gazed down at his plate.

Chapter Fourteen

Billy had always enjoyed a close relationship with his brother-in-law. He looked forward to their daily banter in the yard, even parts of cars that might be thrown at him in jest, and the ability to hurl some back and not get a punch in the face. So when Aron's name-calling, play-fighting and general schoolboy humour began to peter out, Billy started to worry.

A thick fog hung over the yard as he unlocked the main gate on the first Monday morning in November. He shivered and walked quickly to the office. The boiler had already kicked in, and he had two coffees ready by the time he heard Aron's bike roar up.

"Morning." Billy held out a steaming cup towards Aron. "How's it going?"

Aron gave Billy a nod and took the drink over to his desk.

"Cheers."

The silence was unbearable. Billy wracked his brain.

"Okay if I turn on the radio?"

Aron took off his bike gear and had a swig of coffee.

"Whatever you like."

AC/DC blasted out into the icy atmosphere. Billy picked up a pen and held it lengthways in front of his mouth.

"It's a long way to the shop if you want a sausage roll!"

Usually Aron would have joined in or made some other alternative or suggestive lyrics. Billy regarded Aron, head down as he sifted through unopened post.

"Everything all right, mate?"

He turned the radio down a notch as Aron looked up.

"Why wouldn't it be?"

"I just wondered." Billy replied with a shrug. "You don't seem yourself lately."

"Mind your own fucking business."

The first customer of the day drove into the yard. Billy hurried to the door, ran outside and slammed it shut behind him.

***

It was easy to find things to do in the yard. Billy kept himself busy taking saleable parts from unsalvageable cars, and let Aron answer the phone and process paperwork. Around half past eleven his stomach told him it was lunchtime. Billy reluctantly headed for the office, made a point of not looking at Aron, and opened the fridge.

"Sorry mate, I've got things on my mind."

Billy put his lunchbox on his desk and took off the lid before turning towards Aron.

"The baby? Ede and me are chuffed about it. It's a great thing your Ez is doing for us. I want you to know that."

Aron nodded.

"Listen, I know Ede, and she won't want to give it up. There's going to be a shit-storm when it's born."

Billy tried to quell a rising unease.

"No, she wouldn't do that. Eden's even going with her to any doctors' appointments. I don't think you need to worry there."

"Anyway, it should be *my* kid in her belly."

In a flash Billy knew the real reason for Aron's personality change.

"I never went anywhere near her, mate, and *you* know I don't intend to either. By August next year this will all be over and then maybe we can get back to normal."

Aron nodded.

"I've never gone through anything like this before. It's kind of hard for me."

"It's the first time for all of us." Billy took a bite of his sandwich. "We'll make it up as we go along."

He was rewarded with the glimmer of a smile.

"I'm glad you're happy. I can't seem to get my head around it."

Billy bit into a ham sandwich.

"Which bit can't you get your head around?"

"All of it." Aron sighed. "She knows I'm against the whole thing, but hey, it's done now. I've got to suck it up, as they say."

"It'll work itself out."

Billy decided not to dwell on Aron's announcement. Esme was sure to give the baby up. *Hadn't she already said she would?* There was no way she would do anything to hurt her sister. Eden was going to be a mother at last, and that was all there was to it.

Chapter Fifteen

Eden held her sister's hand as the midwife, ultrasound probe in hand, exposed Esme's abdomen.

"I'm Denise Parry, your assigned midwife. I'm going to apply some gel, and then you'll be able to see your baby."

"It's not my baby." Esme kept her eyes averted from the screen and pointed at Eden. "It's hers."

Eden smiled at the midwife, who remained tactfully silent. Tears stung her eyes at the sight of her baby's head and body on display, which had appeared as if by magic. The baby tumbled about joyfully in the cavernous depths of the womb. Eden was mesmerised.

"Can you tell if it's a boy or girl?" She asked with a shaky voice. "I'd like to know."

The midwife looked from Eden back to Esme, whose eyes were closed.

"Is that okay with you, Mrs Jones?"

"Whatever my sister wants."

Denise nodded.

"And will your sister be your birth partner?

"Yes."

Eden squeezed Esme's fingers in appreciation, and looked back to the screen as the midwife spoke.

"It's a girl, and by the measurements I'm getting, you're on course for the end of July, Mrs Jones. Would you like a photo?"

"Just for my sister, not for me."

"I shall print one out. Everything looks fine. The baby is doing very well."

Eden wiped her eyes as Esme sat up and dried her abdomen with some tissue paper.

"Sorry, it was a bit emotional seeing her."

"I was the same with the twins." Esme replied. "Imagine how I felt at seeing *two* heads!"

"It's so *real* now." Eden said excitedly. "Billy and I can start thinking up some names tonight, and now I know what colour wool to buy."

Eden slipped down from the table.

"Aron and I couldn't agree on girls' names for months. All the arguing was a waste of time anyway when two boys popped out. We didn't want to know the sex beforehand."

"What girl's name did you settle on eventually?" Eden took the scan photo from the midwife and stared at it. "Did you want to see this photo, Ez?"

"No. She's totally *your* baby. Aron and I chose Shannon for a girl. I wanted something a little bit unusual, but Aron kept on about traditional names. He gave in, partly because I was so huge and uncomfortable at the end, and I think he felt sorry for me."

Eden chuckled and put the photo in her bag.

"Well, there's only *one* in there now."

"Thank God for that." Esme laughed. "Let me know what names you and Billy choose."

***

She could hardly wait to hear his key turn in the lock. Eden rushed down the hallway and into Billy's surprised arms.

"It's a girl!"

Billy gave her a squeeze.

"So I hear. Ez phoned Aron at lunchtime. Great news."

She grinned and snuggled against his chest.

"We're going to have a daughter."

"Too right." Billy chuckled. "She'll be giving us lip before we know it, and the boys will be beating a path to the front door."

They walked arm in arm to the kitchen.

"Dinner's ready. I've done a turkey casserole and dumplings in the slow cooker." Eden gave Billy's behind a playful slap. "Let's eat and think up some names at the same time."

Billy lifted the hot earthenware pot out of the slow cooker and placed it on the table upon a cork mat.

"What about Claudia?"

Eden pulled a face as she placed a ladle, plates and cutlery in front of Billy.

"Ugh, no. I don't think so. Do you like Estelle?"

"Not especially." Billy lifted the lid of the pot. "There's five dumplings in here."

"You have three, I only want two. What about Celia?"

"Does *she* want one?" Billy added a heaped ladle of food to his plate.

"Not yet." Eden laughed. "Passable?"

Billy shook his head.

"What about Rosemarie?"

"Rosie, yes." Eden took the proffered ladle. "But not Rosemarie."

They ate in companionable silence. Presently Billy helped himself to another plate of food.

"This is a lovely meal, Ede. Just right for autumn nights. What about Justine?"

Eden turned her mouth down at the corners.

"Jessica?"

"Possibly." Billy nodded. "Julia?"

Eden raised a thumb.

"Ah, Julia, after Ms Roberts perhaps?" She gave him a wink. "Yes, I like that one. How about Elswyth?"

"Elswyth?" Billy laughed out loud. "No daughter of mine is going to be called Elswyth! Where the hell did you get that one from?"

"It's the first name of an author my mum used to read. Can't remember her surname, but I like the sound of Elswyth. It's kind of romantic, isn't it?"

"No, it's kind of godawful." Billy ate a whole dumpling. "The kid's got to live with whatever we name her forever."

Eden finished eating, and put down her knife and fork.

"So, we've got Rosie and Julia so far."

"I never said I liked Rosie." Billy wiped his plate clean with a slice of bread. "*You* did."

Eden rolled her eyes briefly upwards.

"*Julia* then."

"Maybe." Billy gave a gentle belch. "I've got to think about it."

"Saffron?"

"No way!"

They washed the dishes and put them away before cuddling together on the settee to watch TV. Eden was convinced she had never felt so happy in her entire life.

Chapter Sixteen

The vomiting was manageable if she could attempt to swallow a biscuit with some tea before she got out of bed. Esme laid on her back in bed, gave Aron a nudge with her elbow, and tried to push away another wave of nausea.

"What?" Aron yawned and turned over on his side. "It's too early to get up."

"Please can you get me some tea and a biscuit, or I think I might upchuck."

"Shit."

The bed creaked as Aron sat up sleepily and rubbed his eyes.

"How long does this go on for?"

She kept as still as she could.

"With the boys it only went after about the fourth month."

"Deep joy."

His footsteps retreated down the stairs and Esme fought back another tsunami of sickness. When she was certain she could not hold out any longer, a welcome cup of tea and a slice of dry toast appeared on a tray.

"We've run out of biscuits."

She sat up slowly, took the tray from Aron and nibbled on one side of the toast.

"What you mean is that you've eaten them all."

"Not me." Aron shrugged and climbed back into bed. "Both boys have developed a liking for custard creams."

Esme felt the nausea receding as she slowly finished the toast.

"Little buggers. I'll have to put the biscuit tin up higher. It's a good thing we won't have to feed three of them. Ede can take over with this one."

Aron leaned back on the pillows and closed his eyes.

"You sure you can give it up?"

"It's a *she*, remember?" Esme took a few sips of tea. "Yes, I can give her up because she belongs to Eden and Billy."

She shuffled along in the bed towards him, and cuddled up to his chest.

"Thanks for the tea and toast. I'm sorry pregnancy affects me like this, but it won't be for long."

She felt an arm snake around her shoulder, and she closed her eyes. She must have gone into a light doze straight away, as Aron's voice floated through to her consciousness seemingly from a distance.

"Do you feel strange that it's Billy's baby in there?"

Wide awake now, she propped herself up on one elbow and looked at him.

"As opposed to yours, you mean?"

Aron kept his eyes firmly shut.

"Er... yeah, I suppose so."

"I don't feel strange." Esme replied. "I feel contented because I've made my sister happy. I've wiped away all the miserable years she's had trying to get pregnant. Have you got a problem with it then?"

"No, no. Not at all."

Esme was unconvinced. She snuggled back down, but froze at sudden giggling from the bedroom next door.

"The boys are awake. I'll go, as it was your turn last Sunday."

She wondered if it was relief that made her husband climb out of bed rather hurriedly.

"No, don't worry, I'll see to them."

***

She always thought of Sundays as quality time with the family. No school runs, no scrapyard, three lazy meals, and trips out as a foursome. So after breakfast when her husband announced that he had bought a rod and line and a day's fishing licence at Needham Lake, Esme pushed back a niggling worry to the back of her mind and tried to focus on the positive.

"It'll bring you and Billy closer together, I'm sure."

"Yeah, we're best buddies." Aron slung a large bag over his shoulder. "See you later."

Chapter Seventeen

Aron decided Billy was right; fishing *was* peaceful. You had a few hours to yourself to zone out and solve any ongoing problems. He looked around the lake; each square jetty contained one man sitting in silent splendour with a rod, line, bait, weather-proof clothes and a portable gas stove. *Were they all weighed down with as many problems as he was?* He could not read their expressions, as their faces, thankfully none of them Billy's, remained impassive.

He cast out into the lake and stared at the ripples from the float widening outwards upon the still water. *Was he being an arsehole for hating the sight of his wife pregnant with another man's child?* Aron sighed; *would all men feel the same as him in a similar situation?*

He shivered as a cold breeze blew around the back of his neck, causing him to pull up the hood of his coat. No fish were nibbling at the bait as yet, and so he lit the one-ring gas cooker and poured out some water for coffee. A train rattled past behind the wall, and he shifted in the foldup chair to get a bit more comfortable. When the kettle boiled, Aron enjoyed a taste of strong black coffee together with the last two custard cream biscuits he had filched from the tin.

A mental image of Esme sporting a distended pregnant abdomen rose to the forefront of his mind. He cast the fishing line out again to the middle of the lake, thinking of the friends he'd been avoiding at the pub, or whose wives would see Ez at the school or walking around the supermarket. He would need to tell the truth to stop all of them arriving at the most obvious but totally incorrect conclusion.

A swan sailed by in graceful serenity. Aron looked for the orange feet paddling frantically beneath the surface, and gave a wry smile. Coffee dregs gone, he likened himself to the swan; calm and composed on the surface, while all the time a rushing torrent of unsettling thoughts were taking place underneath.

He wanted to be able to look at Esme again and enjoy her naked beauty. The twins had made their marks on her skin, but they had been *his* babies. Now another man's seed would distort her body, leaving in its wake another set of stretch marks, piles like grapes, sore lactating breasts like rocks that she would not want him to touch, and whatever damage Billy's baby travelling down her birth canal would do to their sex life.

Yes, that was it, *their sex life*. Aron felt short-changed in the lovemaking department. He remembered the last two months before the twins were born and the weeks afterwards when all his wife had wanted was a cuddle. Another pregnancy would sap her energy, rattle her hormone cage, and push him to the other side of the bed.

Aron threw a pebble as far as he could into the lake. The release of energy was somehow cathartic. He closed his eyes momentarily and took in a deep healing breath. *Was he a selfish bastard who was only thinking of himself?* Whatever his issues, he suddenly realised it was nothing to what Esme would have to go through to give her sister the baby she craved.

The fish were not taking the bait. Another fruitless hour passed. Aron reeled in his line and wondered what his wife and sons were up to. They usually went out on Sundays as a foursome, *so what the hell was he doing sitting by the side of a lake with a load of other sad fuckers?*

***

The house was empty. Aron threw down his bag, pulled his phone from his coat pocket, and tapped in Esme's number.

"Hey, how's the fishes today?"

"Gone to sleep." He sighed. "Didn't catch a thing. I've come home."

"Oh, that's a shame."

"Why?" He replied. "Where are you?"

"We're in the playpark at Needham Lake. We've just had our picnic and then we were going to surprise you a bit later on."

Aron chuckled.

"I'm on my way back, but without the fishing rod."

"Great!" Esme's tinkling laugh was music to his ears. "I didn't fancy going up the climbing frame to rescue Jared when he gets stuck. You *know* he will."

"Yeah, I know." Aron replied. "I'll see you soon."

Chapter Eighteen

She felt better now that the nausea had reduced, and wanted to make the house look good for her Christmas guests. Esme vacuumed and dusted thoroughly, and hung her best red crushed velvet curtains. Aron had erected a 6ft Norwegian spruce, which stood proudly in one corner of the front room and was decorated with tinsel, flashing lights, and every single bauble and do-dad the twins had created since they were able to draw.

Esme was up at 05:30 on Christmas morning to prepare the turkey and put it in the oven. She hummed quietly to herself as she took a bowl of chestnut stuffing from the fridge, made from her grandmother's 1930 recipe. She basted the skin with butter, spread streaky bacon over the turkey's back, stuffed the inside with chestnuts, sage and onion, and covered the whole bird with silver foil. She herself would have preferred to eat a nut roast, but she decided to go with tradition.

"Can we get up now, Mum?"

Two blond heads peered over the bannister. Esme shook her head as she put the turkey in the oven.

"Play in your room for now. When Daddy's awake then we'll get up and open presents."

"Oh…" Jared's voice had a definite whine to it.

"Another hour." Esme looked up at her sons from the kitchen. "I'm going back to bed for a while."

Four feet thundered back upstairs. Esme washed her hands and took two cups of coffee to the bedroom. The boys arguing over which game to play had awoken Aron, who sat up in bed.

"Cheers for the coffee. I hear our little cherubs are already awake."

"Happy Christmas." Esme handed Aron a cup. "I assume you didn't want a lie-in?"

"Even if I did, it doesn't look as though I'm going to get one." He took a quick sip of coffee. "Come and have a quick Christmas cuddle."

She climbed back into bed and snuggled up with a sigh.

"I love you."

He kissed the top of her head.

"I love you too. How are you feeling?"

"I'm all right." She chuckled. "Shall we lock the bedroom door?"

She enjoyed the feel of his hands on her breasts, already slightly swollen.

"Bit risky with those two awake. Let's save it until later. One of them is bound to bash the other one in a minute."

Esme laughed.

"I'm glad you're okay with all this now. I did wonder whether you'd had second thoughts."

There was no reply, which perturbed her somewhat. When a cry sounded from the boys' bedroom, she sighed and gulped down the last of her coffee.

"Come on, Dad. Time to get up."

***

She noticed how her sister's eyes firstly went straight to her abdomen, followed by Billy's.

"That turkey smells delicious!"

"It's nearly done." Esme gave Eden a quick peck on the cheek. "Come in out of the cold. Hello Billy!"

"Happy Christmas!" Billy held out a bag of presents and a bottle of champagne. "Are you allowed any?"

"Try and stop her." Aron shook Billy's hand. "Hi Ede."

"Hi. Merry Christmas."

Esme took the bottle and pulled a face.

"Just a sip to wet the baby's head. Two thousand and eight is going to be a great year."

"Especially around the end of July." Eden replied. "I can't wait."

The bell rang again. James raced downstairs.

"I'll get it, Mum!" He hurled open the door and squealed with delight". "Nanny and Grandad, it's Christmas!"

"Which one is this?" Billy studied his nephew's face with interest. "I can never tell the difference."

"It's James." Esme laughed. "Their ears are slightly different shapes, and Jared is quieter. Hi Mum and Dad, do come in although it's getting a little crowded in the hallway."

Jared, a reading book under one arm, came down the stairs more sedately.

"Can I open my presents now?"

"Yes, we're all here. Everyone, leave your coats over the bannister and come and sit in the front room."

A crackling fire, together with fairy lights on the tree and around the walls gave the room a homely glow. The boys rushed past her and began tearing wrapping paper on their piles of presents. Esme put a hand on each boy's arm.

"Er... what did I tell you about opening presents? We need to write down who sent what so that you can do some thank-you cards."

The expression on both boys' faces showed much disgust. While Aron served dry Sherries, Esme handed out presents from beneath the tree.

"Ede, you'll love your one."

She watched her sister unfold a pile of newborn girls' clothes and hug them to her chest.

"Thanks *so* much! All we need now is little Julia to fill them."

Janet Prentice tore open the wrapping on a bottle of perfume and looked up.

"Thanks Eden. So you've decided on *Julia*?"

"We both like it." Billy replied. "We'll stick with Julia."

Esme felt a twinge of disappointment at the name.

"Okay."

"But you can choose the middle name, Ez." Eden replied. "This baby is a joint effort. I couldn't be a mother without you."

"Ah, thanks for that." Esme laughed. "What about Shannon?"

"Shannon it is." Eden nodded.

Esme, feeling a little brighter, hugged her sister.

"Thanks, and also thanks for my maternity dress, Ede. I don't need it just yet though."

"Mum! Nanny and Grandad gave me ten pounds and some Lego!" James held up the note and waved it about in the air.

"And me!" Jared ran over to Barry and Janet Prentice and gave them a hug. "Thank you!"

Esme left the frenzy of unwrapping and headed out to the peace and quiet of the kitchen. The vegetables were not too soft, the turkey had browned, and a tray of roast potatoes and Yorkshire puddings were ready. She carried 8 warm plates from the bottom of the oven into the dining room, already set with her best silverware for the occasion.

"Can I help you?"

She looked at her sister, happy and healthy once more, and gave silent thanks.

"Sure. You can put the veggies in bowls if you like. Aron can carve the bird at the table."

All the people she loved were together, and she was pregnant at last. She gave a little tweak to the centre flower arrangement, and felt a warm *Lady Bountiful* glow. She could feed her entire immediate and extended family. She could play the genial hostess. She could create a baby for her sister. She was the mother of twins. She was *amazing*.

***

Esme put down her knife and fork and flopped back in her chair.

"Phew! I know I get hungrier when I'm pregnant, but even *I* couldn't eat any more."

"There's Christmas pud to come as well, don't forget." Aron waggled a finger in her direction. "And then mince pies."

"You're eating for two now." Pamela chewed daintily on a roast potato. "By the way, will this be your last pregnancy?"

Esme nodded.

"Oh, yes. Definitely."

She was aware of the older woman's gaze.

"What if Eden wants a brother or sister for *this* one? You could end up becoming a baby machine."

"I wouldn't even *think* of asking Ez for two babies." Eden replied off-handedly. "One is quite enough, to be sure."

Billy, quick on the uptake, butted in.

"Mum! What a question! It's Christmas Day, so be nice."

"Sorry, I'm just thinking of the practicalities. People these days tend to want more than one baby."

Eden, unsmiling, regarded her mother-in-law with the hint of an icy stare.

"How come *you* had only one then?"

She enjoyed Pamela's squirm of embarrassment.

"Leave it, Ede." Billy replied. "Let's just enjoy the day."

Esme held up a cracker towards Aron and made a mental note to have a word with her sister about Pamela.

Chapter Nineteen

At sixteen weeks she felt the first tiny flutterings of life inside her, causing a rush of maternal love to flow through her that she never thought would happen again. *Shannon*; the daughter she'd never had or would ever have again, was alive; a daughter that would even up the gender imbalance in her home. Esme imagined a kindred spirit to have girly chats with whilst baking floury scones and lemon cakes together.

As soon as the baby kicked, Esme would stop whatever she was doing to put her hands on her abdomen and send thought messages to the little person growing like a weed on the nourishing blood from her body. A scan photo would have been concrete evidence that her daughter existed, and Esme now wished that she had asked for one.

When the boys were at school and Aron at the yard, Esme would secretly knit pink bootees, pink and white baby cardigans, and tiny pram suits. She would smile benignly at pregnant ladies in the street and hope her own bump showed large enough to receive an empathetic acknowledgment in return.

But it was all a farce. Sooner or later she would have to hand Shannon over to her sister, and her daughter would become her niece. Esme felt a kick of protest in her belly at the thought of it, as though Shannon was already aware of the unfolding situation.

Why should Shannon be deprived of two older brothers and end up being a lonely, only child? Why should she, Esme, be forced to give up a daughter that she already loved beyond measure?

When she received an appointment for a 20 week mid-term scan, Esme changed it to a day when she knew that Eden had no choice but to work a long shift at the library. Spring was around the corner, and the maternity dress her sister had bought her at Christmas now fitted snugly over an expanding bump. She drove along the A14 and felt a stab of excitement on seeing the Bury St. Edmunds' sugar factory appear in the distance. The hospital was now only a couple of miles away, the hospital where her daughter would make her entrance into the world.

Esme found a space in the front car park and made her way upstairs to the Obstetrics & Gynaecology Department, where several other ladies in various stages of pregnancy were waiting for their names to be called. She took a magazine and tried not to think of Eden's reaction when she received a photo of the scan she had unwittingly missed.

After a short wait, Denise Parry waved her in for bloods, weight and urine tests.

"Hello. Where's your sister today?"

Esme grimaced as she stood on the scales as gently as possible..

"She couldn't get the time off work. Can I have a couple of photos today please? Our mother would like one as well as my sister."

"Of course." Denise nodded. "Your weight is creeping up a little bit. We only like our ladies to put on two stones at the most."

"I know." Esme nodded. "Sorry. I'm so hungry all the time now."

Denise chuckled.

"After all those months of feeling sick, it's like the body's making up for lost time. Have you brought your morning water sample in?"

Esme nodded and fished in her bag.

"Here it is."

"I'll just go and check it, as around twenty weeks there's a slight chance of gestational diabetes. I'll also check for any kind of bladder or kidney infection."

She watched the midwife's expression on her return, but could find no signs of alarm.

"Your sugar levels are fine." Denise announced with a smile. "I'll examine you and take some bloods, and then we can listen to the baby's heartbeat and perform the scan."

The darkened room was somehow peaceful, with a closed door shutting off the hubbub outside. Esme watched an outline of her baby's shape on the screen, and felt reassured on listening to her daughter's strong heartbeat.

"Your sister will be sad to miss this."

She kept her eyes on the screen and wracked her brain for a chance to change the subject.

"It's very fast, isn't it?"

"No, if you remember from last time, one hundred and forty beats per minute is quite normal."

"Good." Esme nodded. "I'll make sure to give Eden a photo, and bring her along next time. "

There was a side pocket in her bag that was just the right size to hold Shannon's first picture. As she wiped the gel from her abdomen, Esme smiled to herself with the realisation that nobody but herself would ever know it was in there.

Chapter Twenty

Eden stared at her daughter's second scan picture with dismay.

"Why didn't you ask me to go with you? I would have liked to see Julia moving about on the screen!"

They were in this together; she couldn't think of any reason why her sister would have gone to the appointment alone. It made no sense after all they had gone through thus far.

She noticed how Esme kept her eyes on the photo.

"They rang me up and said my appointment had been cancelled, but they had another one for yesterday. I knew you had to work because of staff shortages, and so I didn't bother you. Look how she's changed compared to the last one."

It was true. Julia had grown in length. Eden smiled and clutched the photo to her chest.

"She's doing all right then? Heartbeat okay?"

"She's fine." Esme nodded. "Just perfect."

Eden breathed a sigh of relief.

"Always let me know if they change the appointment dates, because I can usually get somebody to swap shifts with. Anyway, I'm giving in my notice at the end of this month, so from April I'll be free to come with you at any time."

"Great."

Esme did not seem as enthusiastic as before, and Eden felt a slight unease that she couldn't quite put her finger on. She decided to put Ez's moodiness down to fluctuating hormones, and remembered how a slight depression had plagued her sister during her previous pregnancy.

"Come on, let's go shopping! I want to buy a pram and a cot, then there's a steriliser to get, a baby bath, and loads of other things. I want to go mad with Billy's credit card in Kiddie World! I'm going to need your advice, sis. I'll drive to Peterborough, and you can sit in the back like the Queen of Sheba."

She was disappointed when Esme shook her head.

"Not today. It's too far, and I have to be back at school by ten to three to get the boys."

"The weekend then?" Eden asked hopefully. "Aron can have the kids and ..."

"I'll see what he's doing." Esme interrupted. "If he's free then I'll come with you."

"Great!" Eden replied with more confidence than she felt. "I'm going to have a lorry load of stuff delivered!"

***

By Friday evening of that week she had still not heard from Esme, and strangely enough there had been no other contact from her sister. Eden, uncharacteristically silent, pushed a few peas around her plate with a knife.

"What's up?" Billy glanced at her as he brought a forkful of fish to his lips. "You look like you've lost a tenner and found five pence."

Eden put down her cutlery.

"It's Ez. She didn't tell me about the scan appointment last Monday, and she hasn't got back to me about going to Kiddie World tomorrow or Sunday."

"She's probably had a row with Aron or something. We can go together on Sunday. I'm working Saturday morning, but we can spend all day there on Sunday if you like? The following weekend I'll get some paint and we can start turning the spare room into a nursery."

She brightened up at his words.

"Okay, great! Ez has been a bit moody lately, although she was like that before with the twins. Perhaps I ought to leave her alone for a few days?"

"Yeah." Billy nodded. "Good idea. Come on, eat up. You're going to have a baby, don't forget."

She laughed and picked up her knife and fork again.

"Yes, I am, aren't I?"

***

She felt a bit of a fraud walking around Kiddie World. In every aisle there were pregnant ladies or mothers with toddlers. Eden looked down at her own flat abdomen and wondered why God in his wisdom had singled her out to be barren.

"Perhaps I should have stuck a cushion up my dress?"

"It might fall down when you were walking about." Billy peered into a pram. "Jeez, have you seen these prices?"

Eden wondered if she would ever work out how to fold down any of the prams to get one in the boot of her car.

"We can afford it, but they all look very complicated contraptions."

"We'll work it out." Billy pointed with a forefinger. "What about that one over there? It's a pushchair, car seat, travel cot and booster seat all in one. I think it might even crack walnuts too.

"And cook the dinner?" Eden chuckled.

"Yeah, while it's feeding the baby at the same time."

She followed his gaze to a dark green *'Ickle Bubba'* pram. The price of £499 seemed reasonable compared to some of the others.

"Yes, I like it."

"Okay, if you're happy with that one we'll take a ticket to the till when we've found a cot. They'll deliver everything, I'm sure."

"Okay."

Fifteen childless years had somewhat reduced her expertise when it came to pushchairs, and she was confused with the myriad of choices on offer. She picked up a purchase ticket.

"Let's find the cot now."

Half of the first floor was given over to various brands of cots and mattresses. She wandered around in a daze seeing Julia, the very image of Billy, stretched out in every cot.

"I think Ez had bamboo mattresses for the twins. I'll get one too."

She was happier now that she knew what she was looking for. A seemingly bored sales assistant was glad to help, and before long she was excited to add a ticket for a *Winnie the Pooh Deluxe Cot Bed* to her list of purchases. Billy took a quick look at the price.

"Apart from the high chair, that'll do for today otherwise we'll be destitute for the rest of the month."

She held on to Billy's arm in the queue to pay, and gave it a squeeze.

"We're going to be parents!"

"We sure are." Billy replied. "And that's a fact."

Eden positively skipped out to the car and smiled at the many pregnant women about. One in particular, huge and obviously near her due date, jogged a distant memory.

"Billy, why did your mum only have one baby? You stopped her from answering my question during the Christmas dinner. I meant to ask you afterwards, but I forgot until now."

Billy activated the central locking system and the SUV's doors clicked open.

"Oh, she doesn't talk about it much, but I had an older brother who died aged only three months old in a cot death. She keeps a photo of him on her bedside table. His name was Oliver."

Eden slid into the passenger seat and looked at Billy in surprise.

"You've never mentioned this before."

"No, well, the subject never came up until now. Mum doesn't usually mention it in general conversation either. It must have been a terrible shock for her. I expect she was relieved when I survived and then didn't want to chance her luck again with another one."

As Billy started the engine and pulled slowly out of the car park, Eden tried to fling the thought of dead babies lying in cots from her mind.

Chapter Twenty One

Aron took a quick glance around the bar. Gary and Ian were already there. He gave them a wave and walked over to where they sat in one corner.

"Whose round is it?"

"Yours, you wanker." Gary held up his middle finger. "Mine's a Guinness."

Ian held up his right thumb.

"Cheers Aron. Pint of lager for me. Ta."

Aron retaliated with a raised middle finger in Gary's direction, and then set off through the crowded pub. After a longer than usual wait he returned with three drinks and some bags of crisps on a tray, then sat down and shuffled off his jacket.

"Cheers fellas." Aron took a long swig of bitter. "How's it going?"

Gary spoke through a white frothy Guinness moustache.

"We're okay, but you never told us you were going to be a daddy again. Sue saw Ez in Sainsbury's. You kept that quiet, you sly old fox."

Aron chuckled.

"Actually, I'm not."

He noticed the look pass between his friends, and just to be mischievous kept the awkward silence going until Gary decided to speak.

"How's that then? Er…"

"Ez is doing it for her sister. Billy's the daddy, not me."

"Sounds dodgy, mate." Ian drew in a sharp breath. "Your Ez going to give it up then?"

Aron nodded.

"Yeah, the girls have it sorted between them. She's nearly six months gone now. Ez has to register the birth, and then Billy and Ede will fill out a parental order form for the court. They've got six months to fill out the form to be the legal parents, but knowing Eden she'll do it straight away."

Ian finished half of his pint of lager before speaking.

"How long have we been mates, Aron?"

Aron bit off the top of a packet of crisps.

"Since Year Ten when I saw you looking down Miss Taylor's cleavage."

"Yeah, she was well developed, wasn't she?" Ian laughed. "And I've known Ez for about eleven years. So I'm asking again…will there be trouble if she has to give the kid up?"

Aron shook his head.

"Maybe if she wasn't doing it for her sister, but I'm sure she won't let Eden down. I know her better than anyone."

Ian raised the palms of both hands.

"Fair enough, mate, but I wouldn't touch that with a barge pole."

"Me neither." Gary added earnestly. "Sue said Ez never spoke about anything like that. She took it as a normal pregnancy."

"Probably wanted to keep it to herself." Aron shrugged. "I don't think she's told anybody. Anyway, are we going to see Ipswich play on Saturday or not?"

"What's the point?" Gary laughed. "The Canaries will win again, but all right, we might as well. We can meet up at Portman Road an hour before the match and get a few bevvies in."

"Suits me." Ian nodded. "And it'll be *your* round, Gary."

Gary laughed and took a packet of crisps.

"Fuck off. Daddy here's celebrating. He can cough up."

"I'm not the Daddy." Aron rolled his eyes. "I've already told you."

"Yeah, that's what they all say, mate." Gary held up his glass. "Cheers!"

***

The front room light was still on as Aron turned the key in the lock, walked inside, and gave Esme a kiss on the cheek.

"Hey, I didn't expect to see you still up."

"You stink of beer." Esme yawned and switched off the TV. "Did you say anything to them? I didn't want to tell Sue all the ins and outs of it, and so I thought I'd leave it to you."

Aron nodded.

"Yeah, they all know now. It'll go around like wildfire. We won't need to tell anybody else. Ez..."

"What?"

He hesitated for a moment before replying.

"Gary and Ian reckon you might want to keep the baby."

"I've said to Eden that I'll give her up, and I will."

She did not quite meet his eyes, and Aron, mindful of Ian's words, felt the first inkling of a possible future tidal wave of emotional torment.

Chapter Twenty Two

By the time the summer heat returned at the end of May, Esme felt bloated, hot, and as big as the side of a house. After she dropped the boys off at school she had to force herself to clean the house, visit the supermarket, and prepare an evening meal. The highlight of her day came when she had time to sit in the garden, feel Shannon kicking against her ribs, and be able to silently commune with her baby.

Visits from Eden, no longer gainfully employed, had increased in frequency and were totally unwelcome. On a scorching hot day in early June, Esme opened the front door and forced a smile.

"Hi Ede. I'm just sitting in the garden."

She leaned back as Eden pushed past her into the hallway.

"Well, you carry on sitting there and I'll get you a nice cold drink."

She could not be bothered to make small talk. Esme waddled back out into the garden and made herself comfortable on a sun lounger.

"We're not alone anymore, little one."

There was an answering kick, and her stomach rolled and pitched enough to make her feel slightly queasy. Languidly, she put her hands on her abdomen and closed her eyes.

"Hush."

"Oh! I can see her moving!"

An uninvited hand pressed down on her belly. Esme opened her eyes, shifted away slightly, and took the proffered drink.

"Thanks."

She drank thirstily, but was aware of Eden's stare.

"Are you okay?"

"Yes, I'm fine." Esme sat up as much as she could. "Just tired, that's all."

"It's the heat." Eden nodded. "Why don't you go and lie down and I'll collect the boys from school today?"

Esme gave a thin smile and heaved herself off the sun lounger.

"That'll be great. Sorry not to be very good company."

"Don't worry." Eden shook her head. "I can see how uncomfortable you are carrying Julia about in this heat. I've brought my knitting, so I'll sit here and finish this little hat and then I'll go and get the boys."

Without another word, Esme went upstairs, drew the curtains, and sank down gratefully upon the bed. She rested her hands on her abdomen again.

"You're *mine*, little Shannon, *mine*."

The baby gave a kick of agreement. Esme grinned to herself.

"Nobody is going to take you away from me."

***

She awoke to the noise of both boys racing each other up the stairs, and Eden's loud hiss of disapproval from below.

"Shhh!"

The bedroom door flew open as James rushed in.

"Are you ill, Mummy?"

Jared followed behind his brother more sedately. Esme sat up and smiled at two pairs of inquisitive grey eyes.

"No, I'm not ill. The baby makes me tired and hot. I just had a little doze, but I'll get up now."

"How did it get in there?"

Esme's heart sank.

"Eh?"

"The baby. How did it get in there, Mummy?"

Esme looked at two earnest faces.

"It grew from a seed. That's all you need to know at the moment."

Mollified, the boys rushed along the landing to play in their bedroom. Esme looked at her watch and was surprised to find she had slept for the best part of two hours. An arm holding a steaming mug snaked around the door, followed by her sister's grinning face.

"Cup of tea, sleeping beauty!"

"Oh, thanks." Esme took the mug and tried to mask her annoyance at Eden's cheerfulness. "I'll come down. I'll need to start dinner soon."

"Tell me what you want and I'll get it ready. I finished Julia's little hat by the way."

I want you to go home!

"Super. She'll have more clothes than the pair of us put together."

Eden laughed.

"Can I do anything else for you?"

"No, it's fine." Esme shook her head. "You get home. Billy will be back soon. I'm okay."

"Only if you're sure?" Eden replied with concern. "I'll be back tomorrow to help out anyway."

Esme shook her head.

"You don't have to come every day. Really."

She forced a smile on receiving a peck on the cheek.

"What else have I got to do? I've given up work, you're carrying my daughter, and it's the least I can do to help you out."

A wall of heat hit her as she went downstairs and opened the front door.

"See you tomorrow then."

"Absolutely!" Eden trilled. "You'll be sick of me by the time Julia's born!"

Esme waved. In her opinion, her sister had never spoken truer words. She was heartily sick of the sight of her already, and she still had another two months to go.

***

"Everything okay? You haven't said a word all the time we've been washing up."

Esme put the last plate on the drainer and pulled the plug from the sink.

"Oh, sorry Aron. It's just that Eden's here all the time and I'm not getting any chance to be by myself."

Aron took the wet plate and dried it with a tea towel.

"She's excited. What do you expect?"

Esme sighed.

"Do you think she'll take it the wrong way if I tell her to not come round so often?"

"She's bound to." Aron nodded. "You're pregnant with her daughter. Wouldn't you do the same if the shoe was on the other foot?"

He had a point. Esme decided there was nothing else but to put up with it. Circumstances would change soon enough.

Chapter Twenty Three

Eden stepped back and admired four pale pink walls that contrasted nicely with a frieze of smiling multi-coloured teddy bears running just below the ceiling.

"Do you like my handiwork, Billy?"

She smiled at him as he looked up from poring over a set of instructions.

"Yeah, great. I'll have this cot set up in no time."

She took in a deep breath of excitement.

"I still can't believe we're going to be parents in just six weeks' time."

She sat down in the brand new rocking chair that had been delivered a few days previously, and reached over to open a drawer in the baby changing table stuffed full of disposable nappies. She took out a nappy and waved it in the air.

"It's like a dream come true."

He grinned at her and laid out pieces of cot on the carpet.

"She'll soon be screaming her lungs out at two o'clock in the morning."

"I don't care." Eden sighed and replaced the nappy. "I just want to hold her in my arms. I think Ez is getting cheesed off with being pregnant though. She's moody. Funnily enough, I don't remember her being like that with the twins for as long as this. She was okay after the first few months."

"Probably the heat." Billy shrugged. "It gets everyone down I would think, especially pregnant women."

Eden nodded.

"Yes of course, the boys were born in the winter. Do you think we've got everything ready now? We've got the steriliser and bottles, tins of milk, dummies, nappies, clothes, the swinging thing that clips to the doorframe, a stair gate, a low chair and a high chair."

"Apart from this cot and the mobile which I'll do in a minute, then...yeah." He replied, and took a screw out of the corner of his mouth. "Christ, all these things we have to buy to stop her doing anything! Didn't Ez offer you her old stuff?"

She shook her head.

"No, but then again I'd rather have everything new."

"Yeah, but I'm not Bill Gates, honey."

She laughed as the cot took shape before her eyes. After Billy added the mattress she stood up and went over to the single wardrobe, pulled out the drawer underneath and took out padded surrounds, a freshly washed fitted sheet and a pink fluffy blanket.

"I can't wait to make up Julia's bed!"

She lovingly tied padding around the cot, pulled the sheet in place over the mattress, and tucked the blanket neatly over the sheet then stood with Billy looking down at the empty bed.

"We just need some toys now and pictures on the walls for her to look at."

"How about some homely slogans like '*Always live within your means*'?

She giggled, but Billy's previous throwaway remark had suddenly struck home. *Why had Ez not offered her the high chair, cot, and other baby paraphernalia that she knew was still in her sister's loft?* As far as she knew, they had only sold one high chair, one cot, and the double buggy. *Why were they still holding on to baby stuff they would never use again? Sentimental reasons perhaps?* Otherwise it made no sense at all.

Chapter Twenty Four

For once the boys and Shannon were quiet. A blond head rested on both of her upper arms, and the baby had ceased kicking long enough to listen to her read a bedtime story. Esme, now unable to sit upright, slouched back on the settee and was grateful she knew the words of the story off by heart.

"...and they all lived happily ever after."

Fat chance of that.

She looked over to where Aron pressed buttons on the remote and scrolled through TV channels.

"The boys are ready for bed, love."

She put her arms around their thin shoulders, and gave each one a squeeze.

"Sleep tight, little boys. Don't let the bedbugs bite."

Jared looked up at her, his expression serious.

"Mummy, I don't want you to give the baby to Aunty Eden."

"And I don't either." James piped up and kicked the bottom of the settee with his heels. "She's *our* baby."

She kissed the top of their heads.

"Aron!"

"Yeah, yeah." He placed the remote on the seat of his armchair and stood up. "Come on lads, time for bed. It's Aunty Eden's baby, not ours. You'll still see her whenever you want, I'm sure."

The usual noisy protests took place, but tonight it seemed to her as though the boys were unwilling to leave the warmth and safety of her embrace. Esme closed the book, kissed her sons' warm foreheads, and wished she could hold them aged eight forever. Aron gave her a wink, tucked one squealing boy under each arm, and ran full pelt up the stairs. Bedtime routine completed, he returned to the front room where Esme held out a mug of tea in his direction.

"Cheers. The little buggers don't seem tired tonight."

"That's because you wind them up just before bedtime."

He laughed.

"That's what dads do, isn't it?" He took a sip of tea and sat down beside her. "They asked again about the baby."

Esme ignored a sinking feeling in her stomach.

"Did they?"

"Yeah." Aron replied. "*You* don't want to give it up either, do you?"

She shook her head.

"In all honesty, no. Of course she's my baby, but I've promised her to Eden and I aim to stand by that promise."

"I bloody well knew it!" Aron's voice increased in strength. "That's why you're so moody! There's going to be an absolute *shitstorm* next month!"

"No there isn't." Esme replied in a softer tone. "Granted, I didn't feel this way until she started kicking, but I could never face Ede or Billy or my mum and dad again if I kept hold of her."

She leaned towards him and let the tears fall that had been dammed up for so long.

"I don't really want her coming to the house. Every time I see her I think of her holding Shannon, and it's tearing me up inside."

"They've named it Julia, haven't they?" His head rested against her own. "Honey, you've got to stop this. She's Billy's baby... Billy and Ede's."

"Yes I know." She sniffed. "But I *can't* stop. When I talk to the baby, she kicks, and when I ask her to let me sleep, then she does. She's listening to me, Aron. She's part of me. I've bonded with her, and it's the kind of mother and baby bond that will never be broken."

His lack of reply told her he was unable to fix the situation she had mistakenly orchestrated. She felt suffocated by the silence and oppressive heat in the room, and decided then and there that she would happily give her right arm if only she could turn back the clock.

***

The end of school summer term coincided with the start of her Braxton-Hicks contractions. Esme was glad to leave Eden watching the boys in the children's play area while she took the lift upstairs to what she hoped would be her last ante-natal appointment. She walked slowly now, feeling the baby's weight pushing down upon her perineum as though it might at any moment make a splash of an entrance upon the polished hospital corridor. She got to her feet with difficulty when Denise Parry called her name.

"Hello Mrs Jones. Do follow me."

The examination was uncomfortable, and Shannon writhed about, trying to move in an increasingly confined space. Esme let out a deep breath.

"I wish it was all over."

Denise nodded.

"You haven't got long now, I can feel you're having little contractions already. I always tell all my ladies there's one sure way to get that baby out a little bit sooner."

Esme glanced at her in surprise.

"Drink gin and have a hot bath?"

"I wouldn't advise that." Denise laughed. "Just go home and jump on your partner. A night of passion will bring on labour, no problem."

"You've got to be joking!" Esme regarded Denise incredulously. "Look at me! Sex is the last thing on my mind!"

"Well, don't say I didn't advise you." Denise smiled. "But anyway, you're doing okay. Blood tests and pressure and urine test normal. Next time I see you it will probably be on the Central Delivery Suite if my shifts and your labour coincide."

"I hope they do." Esme replied. "I really hope so."

She walked slowly down the stairs towards the front of the hospital, all the while her mind turned cartwheels in an effort to think up a plausible excuse to keep her sister out of the labour room.

Chapter Twenty Five

She awakened suddenly from sleep in the sure and certain knowledge that labour had begun. She moved over from the wet sheet underneath her buttocks, and heaved herself into a sitting position.

"Aron, wake up."

A sleepy voice mumbled from the depths of his pillow.

"What?"

"My waters have broken. The baby's coming a week early. I'll phone Mum and tell her to come over and sit with the boys."

She climbed awkwardly out of bed and threw off the duvet to expose a large pool of amniotic fluid. Aron, more awake now, rubbed his eyes.

"Aren't I supposed to stay here with the twins and you go with Eden?"

"No." Esme shook her head. "I want you with me, like last time. I don't want Eden there. When Mum gets here then we'll go."

As she dialed her mother's number she felt the first gentle hardening of her abdomen. A voice thick with sleep came down the line.

"Ez, are you okay?"

"The baby's started Mum, so I need you to stay with the boys. Don't tell Eden though. I just want to go with Aron."

"I'm on my way." Janet Prentice replied, more awake now, "but Eden will be so disappointed. She's been talking about the birth for months."

Esme gave a *tut* of annoyance.

"She'll get over it. You can tell her later when it's all over. I need Aron with me. I'll ring you when the baby's here."

She ended the call abruptly and went into the en-suite to wash and dress as quickly as possible in-between mild contractions coming about every five minutes. Suitably attired in sandals and Eden's sundress, Esme walked carefully down the stairs followed by Aron clutching her suitcase.

"My mouth is like a soap-boilers arse turned inside out and whitewashed." He yawned. "Have I got time to make a cup of tea?"

She chuckled despite the pains.

"Where on earth did you get that one from? Two sugars in mine please. I need a boost but I'd better not eat anything."

***

She felt every bump in the road. Esme closed her eyes and willed the journey to end.

"This isn't right. " Aron shook his head. "Ede should be driving you. It's what you two arranged."

"The situation's altered now." Esme winced. "I need your arms to rub my back like last time. Okay I had a bruise the size of a dinner plate on my back the day after the twins were born, but it helped with the pain. Eden's arms are like two strands of spaghetti."

The A14 was virtually empty. She felt Aron pick up speed and in no time the sign for West Suffolk Hospital came into view. Esme breathed a sigh of relief along Hardwick Lane.

"Just drive straight to A&E and leave the car outside. You can run out and park it when I'm on the ward."

She hadn't sat in a wheelchair since Aron had pushed her out into the fresh air a day after giving birth to the twins. Esme clutched her abdomen protectively as she heaved herself out of the car then flopped down into the chair outside A&E.

"We'll have to go upstairs in the lift. The Delivery Suite is on the first floor."

The darkened hospital corridors were unusually quiet and for once there was no queue for the lift. Esme pushed the bell for the Delivery Suite and groaned quietly as a new contraction hit.

"Can I help you?"

"It's Esme Jones. I'm in labour."

The door clicked open. A midwife that she had not seen before smiled as she regarded her from behind the reception desk.

"Hello Esme, I'm Ann Pritchard, the midwife in charge. I'm just going to print out your notes." She tapped a keyboard. "Ah...here we are. It says your birth partner is Mrs Eden Reece."

"No, she can't make it." Esme winced and briefly closed her eyes. "My husband here...Aron Jones ...will stay with me." She reached back to touch Aron's fingers.

Aron squeezed her hand.

"I'm just going to park the car now before I get a clamp. I'll be back in a minute with your bag."

Esme nodded and levered herself out of the chair.

"Come with me." Ann beckoned with one finger. "I'll show you to your room."

Shannon kicked, eager to be out of her constrictions. Esme made her way to a comfortable-looking armchair next to a high bed, and sank down gratefully. Ann clipped a board to the end of the bed.

"If you'd like to get into the gown provided and lie on the bed, then I'll be back in a few minutes to examine you and take a few more details. Have your waters broken?"

"Yes." Esme replied, unwilling to move. "Contractions are about every four minutes."

"Good." Ann nodded. "Sounds like you're well on the way. Would you like any pain relief?"

Esme shook her head.

"No, I'm going to try and do without it, and I definitely don't want an epidural."

"Yes, Denise has added that to your notes." Ann took another look at the clipboard at the bottom of the bed. "There's pethidine and gas and air if you choose."

"No, no, I don't want anything. Will I see Denise at all?"

Ann shook her head.

"Denise isn't due back at work until the day after tomorrow."

Left alone and with a slight feeling of dismay, Esme struggled out of her clothing and donned the hospital gown. Through the glass panel in the door she could see Aron and Ann in conversation. Ann came back in and gave Esme a smile.

"I'll see how far you're dilated, and then your husband can come back in."

Ann drew a privacy curtain. Esme gritted her teeth ready for the hated internal examination, and hoped she didn't have another contraction at the same time.

"Four centimetres dilated." Ann snapped off her rubber gloves and pushed the curtain back. "Yes, you're in active labour. I'll put a monitor around your middle so that we can keep an eye on the baby's heartbeat. I'll also need to test your urine and your blood sugar levels, but after that I'll leave you and your husband alone for a while. You can always buzz if you decide you need any pain relief. How long was your last labour?"

"Sixteen hours." Esme took a deep breath and let it out slowly. "Twins."

Ann smiled.

"This one will be a doddle then. I'd say your baby will be here by breakfast time."

"A doddle?" Esme winced. "It'll still be like trying to push a watermelon through a garden hose."

She grimaced at Aron as he strode in with her overnight bag.

"Can you see if you can get my hot water bottle filled please? It might help if I put it on my lower back. The pains are coming from there, just as they did last time. I've got something like a *retro* womb, I think."

"Sure." He unzipped the case and took out the bottle. "Be back in a tick."

Two hours had gone by in a flash since her rude awakening. Esme sighed and called upon her steely reserve, powers of endurance, and Aron's support to get her through the rest of the night.

    ***

The overly-large clock on the wall opposite read 03:38. She sat on the side of the bed and buried her head in the front of Aron's shirt, now damp with sweat.

"Rub my lower back as hard as you can."

She closed her eyes and enjoyed the pressure of his hands as they took the edge off her pain.

"Not long now honey." Aron grunted with exertion. "You're nine centimetres. Ann said it'll soon be over."

Esme exhaled into his chest.

"I'm so glad you're here. Eden couldn't have done what you're doing."

"She'll be pissed off." Aron kissed the top of Esme's head. "You'll have some explaining to do."

Her sister's angst was nothing to her now, as relentless waves of pain, one after another, screamed through her lower back, lasting a good 45 seconds. She dug her nails into Aron's shoulders, aware of Ann Pritchard's voice sounding close to her left ear.

"I think I need to examine you again, Mrs Jones. You may be ready to push quite soon."

Almost at the same time as Ann spoke, Esme soon felt a familiar pressure on her bowels, a deep and urgent call for release that was impossible to ignore.

"The baby's coming." She lay back against the pillows. "I've got to push!"

"Not yet!" Ann stated firmly. "I have to check. Pant away like you've just run a marathon."

Esme screamed and grabbed Aron's hand as Ann inserted a gloved finger into her vagina.

"Okay, yes, you can push! Come on, give it all you've got!"

She felt out of control of the pain as another powerful contraction deleted any thought in her head except bringing Shannon into the world. She clutched at both knees with her hands, brought them up towards her chest, and pushed with all her might.

"That's it, honey!" Aron supported her shoulders as best he could. "You can do it!"

Esme, exhausted but relieved at now being able to take an active part, watched Ann Pritchard put on a protective gown over her uniform and bring a tray of instruments closer to the bed.

"Time your pushes to go with each contraction, Mrs Jones."

She could smell the blood-sweat-and-tears earthiness of the room. Esme looked up at the clock, 05:26; birds singing for all they were worth outside, and Shannon's head descending into the birth canal. She could hear a kind of animalistic grunting coming from her very core. She cared of nothing else except getting her daughter out of her body.

One scream and almighty push at 06:04 and Shannon's wet head slid out from between her legs. Esme panted as Ann delivered the shoulders.

"One last push Mrs Jones!"

She grabbed hold of Aron, tearing a seam of his shirt in the process.

"I can't do it anymore!"

"Yes you can, baby." Aron lifted up her shoulders. "One more…"

She turned her face into his chest and pushed with all her might, and at 06:10 on Monday July 22nd 2008 she was safely delivered of the daughter she had wanted for so many months. Esme, tearful and weak with tiredness, held out her arms as Ann cut the cord and wrapped the 7lb 15 oz baby in a towel.

"She has your looks, Mrs Jones. I'm going to inject some Oxytocin into your thigh to help deliver the afterbirth."

Esme did not even feel the injection. Euphoric, she looked down with relief tinged with a slight disappointment at the sight of her daughter's ginger hair. Shannon, eyes still closed, sported a tuft of red hair the same colour as Billy's, but with a nose and mouth the same shape as her own.

"Oh my darling!" Esme cried. "You are just perfect!"

"Cough for me, Mrs Jones. We need to deliver the afterbirth." Ann held out a kidney bowl. "You're going to need a couple of stitches as I had to perform an episiotomy, and so there'll be a bit of a wait for the doctor, but otherwise you're fine."

Esme, spent and puzzled that she had felt no pain on being cut, relaxed and let the pillows take her weight.

"No visitors please" She stated firmly. "I want it to be just myself, Aron and the baby."

She looked at Aron for confirmation, who for some unknown reason did not seem quite as joyful as he had been at the birth of his sons. Esme kissed the top of Shannon's warm head, and felt her family was now complete.

Chapter Twenty Six

Eden yawned, stretched, and looked over at the clock; 07:35. She gently prodded her husband's sleeping form by her side.

"Billy, you'll be late for work. The alarm didn't go off."

There was an unintelligible murmur from beneath the sheet. Eden sat up and rubbed her eyes.

"Come on, we've got to get up. Ez will wonder where I've got to."

She shuffled into her slippers and threw on a dressing gown. As she walked out onto the landing she could not resist a quick glance into the pristine nursery next door.

"You'll be with us in no time, little one."

She could hear the floorboards creak as Billy got out of bed. Eden ran lightly down the stairs, already buoyed with the knowledge that their daughter would soon be home. She flicked on the kitchen light, filled up the kettle, and shoved two pieces of bread into the toaster. Billy appeared in the doorway, hair askew.

"Haven't got time for breakfast."

"Cup of coffee?" She switched on the kettle. "Your lunch box is in the fridge."

"Okay." He nodded and pulled out one of the high stools. "Thanks for the sarnies. Shall I bring a take-away home if you're back late tonight?"

The toaster popped. Eden spread some margarine on the toast and added some coffee to two cups.

"If you like. Poor old Ez is just sitting around now waiting for Julia to arrive. I don't like to leave her until Aron gets home. I think the boys are too much for her at the moment."

Coffee made, she sat down next to Billy and chewed her toast thoughtfully.

"I suppose you'll take two weeks' paternity leave?"

"I hadn't really thought about that." Billy looked at her, surprised. "It'll mean leaving Aron alone, but I suppose he'll cope. Maybe just a week though?"

"Okay." She nodded in agreement. "We're going to need some time together with Julia to adjust."

***

As soon as she rang the doorbell she could hear the thunder of the twins' feet down the stairs. James' head appeared around the door and she smiled at him.

"I've come to help Mummy again." Eden smiled at her nephew. "Can I come in?"

James kept the front door half closed.

"Mummy isn't here."

She felt a pang of anxiety at his words. Her mother's footsteps sounded along the hallway, and the door opened fully.

"Why isn't Ez here, Mum? Where is she?"

She looked past her mother, expecting to see Esme waddling along behind, but only the twins were visible.

"Er… she phoned me during the night. She thought she might be in labour. Aron took her to the hospital about one o'clock this morning."

Eden's heart pounded in her chest at her mother's guarded reply.

"But *I* was supposed to be her birth partner!"

Her mobile buzzed with an incoming message. Still standing on the front porch, she read Billy's message with a sickening thud.

'Aron's turned up at the yard, knackered. Baby was born three hours' ago. Weren't you supposed to be there?"

She gazed sightlessly at her mother, open mouthed, with her mind in a turmoil at his words.

"Why didn't you phone me, Mum? I told Ez to phone me any time of the day or night! Why didn't she phone me? It doesn't make any sense!"

"Come in." Janet Prentice beckoned with one hand. "Don't stand on the step. She probably didn't want to bother you in the middle of the night in case it was a false alarm. The baby wasn't due for another week."

She took comfort at her mother's words, unwilling to consider any other alternative.

"I'll go straight to the hospital." Eden shook her head. "She'll need me and I want to cuddle Julia."

Before her mother could reply, she had turned on her heel and was on the way back to her car.

***

The corridors were busy with lost patients on the lookout for clinics, doctors on their way to appointments, secretaries with armfuls of notes, and phlebotomists with their trollies containing test tubes and needles. Eden pushed past them all on her way upstairs to the Central Delivery Suite. Panting slightly, she rang the bell.

"Can I help you?"

The dispassionate, disembodied voice irritated her. Esme tugged at the door which refused to budge.

109

"I'm Esme Jones' birth partner. Please can you let me in. Thanks very much."

She was happy that her voice sounded authoritative enough, and she pulled the door handle again even though she had not heard any answering buzz.

"I'm sorry. That won't be possible right now."

Eden was filled with an uncharacteristic anger.

"But the baby is my daughter! Esme is my surrogate! I want to see my daughter!"

The voice, still calm, carried on.

"Mrs Jones is resting now, and she has stated that she does not want any visitors. I'm sorry, but I cannot be of any more help to you."

"Would you tell her that…"

There was a click, and then silence. Impotent, she stood transfixed and stared at the intercom as though by some miracle the speaker might have had second thoughts. Visions of her daughter crying with hunger whilst Esme slept tortured her mind. Eden pulled her phone from her bag and tapped in Esme's number that she knew off by heart.

"The person you have called is not available. Please leave your name and number after the tone."

Eden kicked the barrier between her and Julia, and let a sob escape from her lips. She found Aron's contact details and tapped on his number. A pleasant but weary-sounding baritone came down the line.

"Hello Eden, I thought you'd be ringing me."

"What's going on?" She could not keep the panic out of her voice. "They won't let me into the ward, and tell me that Ez doesn't want any visitors!"

"She's asleep now. The baby's fine, but she just wants to be left alone for a while. She's tired. She'll be home tomorrow I expect. I'm at the yard at the moment, but I'm going home soon to have a shower and a sleep. Your mum's looking after the boys. We're both knackered."

She picked up on his unwillingness to discuss any further details. Disappointed beyond belief, Eden turned on her heel and in a kind of stupor made her way back to the car. When she pulled up on her driveway she was rather perturbed to discover that she could not remember any part of the journey home. She opened the front door, kicked off her shoes, and then slammed the door shut. She walked dazedly to the bottom stair, and then plonked herself down on it and sobbed.

Chapter Twenty Seven

After just an hour's doze, Esme lay wide awake, too excited to sleep. She turned on her side and stared at the miracle that was Shannon. She wanted the clock to stop so that she could savour the moment forever. Her little daughter slumbered on in her plastic cot, regardless of the upset that her birth would undoubtedly cause as soon as they left the safe confines of the hospital ward. She had a sudden mental image of a pile of shit hitting a fan and distributing itself all around the ward.

Breakfast arrived, a concoction possibly ordered by the previous incumbent. Esme sat up and wolfed down a bowl of porridge, a yoghurt, and a pot of prunes. She felt energised and ready for whatever the day would throw at her; in fact she already had a good idea what would happen. Eden; the sister who was ready to steal *her* baby, would be on the warpath. No way could she, Esme, ever bear to part with such a precious gift.

She reached over into the cot and touched Shannon's tiny fingers. The baby yawned and snuffled momentarily. Esme sat up, swung her legs over the bed, and gently lifted her prize from the cot. The feel of a warm little body in her arms suffused her with maternal pride and a kind of feral protective instinct. She kissed her daughter's forehead.

"Mummy will keep you safe, little one."

Out of the corner of her eye she could see the consultant had started her rounds, accompanied by a group of trainee doctors and the ward manager. Esme clutched Shannon as they came towards her. The consultant picked up s clipboard at the end of her bed.

"Good morning, Mrs Jones. How are you feeling today?"

"Fine, I think." Esme smiled at the group of doctors. "Better than I did last time even."

The consultant flipped through charts on the clipboard.

"I'll pull the curtains around so that I can examine you. If all is well, then you'll be able to go home after lunch. I'll give you some paperwork so that you can register the birth. Is baby feeding all right?"

"Yes." Esme nodded. "I've put her to the breast for some colostrum, and she's had one bottle so far. I've already made an appointment for tomorrow to register the birth."

She laid the baby back down and prepared for the inevitable but necessary loss of dignity.

***

"Is she outside, Aron?"

Esme, nervous, hung on to Aron's arm and walked slowly behind the nurse carrying her daughter.

"Who, Eden?

"Yeah." She nodded. "I can't face her at the moment."

Aron sighed

"I didn't see her when I parked the car. You're going to *have* to meet with her sooner or later. Ez, you've *got* to give that baby up like you promised."

"I know, I know." She replied. "I just want a couple of days with her, that's all."

The nurse reached the main entrance, and then held the baby in outstretched arms.

"Goodbye, Mrs Jones. Enjoy your little girl."

"I will." Esme took the baby. "Thank you."

The heat hit her as soon as she stepped out onto the pavement. Esme blinked, looked down and turned Shannon's face away from the sun. Beside her she heard Aron take a deep breath.

"Hi Eden."

She momentarily closed her eyes at his words, unwilling to emerge from the hospital's tight cocoon. Shannon stirred in her arms, whilst Esme's heart pounded a rhythm in her chest. She clutched the baby tighter. Eden unsmiling, jumped up from a bench just outside the entrance.

"I think I have a right to see my daughter! Why are you trying to stop me? Why was I not allowed to be at the birth?"

Esme stared at her sister, momentarily lost for words. Patients passing through the automatic doors looked on with interest. She felt great relief when Aron stepped in-between them.

"Ede, I don't think this is the right time. Esme's tired. We just want to get home."

"Ez!" Eden's voice rose a couple of semitones and she scooted to the side of Aron. "What on earth's going on? *I* am supposed to take the baby home!"

Her sister stood inches away, straining to get hold of Shannon. Esme pulled a shawl further over the tell-tale red tuft and said the first thing that came into her head.

"And you will, but first I need to take her to register the birth."

Mollified, Eden's demeanour changed. She nodded.

"I'll come with you. Can I see her?" She peered closer into the shawl. "She has Billy's red hair!"

Esme, desperate, began to walk.

"No, only Aron and I are allowed to do it. I'll see you tomorrow." She gave the baby to Aron and held on to the railing leading down to the car park. "We need to go now."

She hurried as fast as a newly delivered mother could manage.

"Julia Shannon, don't forget!" Eden called after her. "Julia Shannon Reece!"

***

The excitement of the previous couple of days had waned. Esme felt weak and was glad of her parents' offer to babysit. With Shannon safely ensconced in the back, she struggled out of the passenger seat of Aron's car and then looked at him.

"I won't be long. After I've registered the birth and you've taken me home, you can go back to work if you like. Mum's there to help."

"I might do that." He nodded. "I don't like to leave it all to Billy for too long. When are you going to hand the baby over to them?"

"Soon."

She was glad of the chance to sit down in the cool foyer of the old council offices and wait her turn to be seen. When the registrar called her name, Esme followed him into a small room and handed over her ID and the hospital's paperwork.

"I'd like to register my baby's name as Shannon Julia Jones please."

Her sister's features came to the forefront of her mind. Esme blinked them away.

Chapter Twenty Eight

She was prepared to stand in the garden all day long until Esme answered the door. Eden gave Billy a nervous grin as they sheltered from the heat in the porch.

"Wait until you see her... she has your red hair, Billy!"

"Something about this whole thing is strange." Billy replied. "The way they've treated you is totally wrong, and Aron's not saying much either. I'm going to get to the bottom of this."

She tapped again on the knocker, whilst hearing the twins' shrill voices behind the door as they spoke to her mother.

"Mum! It's Eden! Can you open the door please?"

She heard the inside bolt shoved back. Her mother's face appeared in the doorway.

"Hi Eden, Billy." Janet Prentice smiled. "It's all a bit chaotic here."

"We want to see our daughter." Eden stepped into the hallway. "I think it's only right, don't you?"

"Of course."

Eden thought her mother seemed unusually guarded. With Billy and the twins following, she went into the front room.

"Where's Ez?"

"She's asleep upstairs." Janet replied. "I expect she'll be down soon with Shannon."

"No, not Shannon...*Julia*." Eden shook her head. "The baby's name is *Julia*."

"Aunty Ede, we've got a new sister!" James declared with pride. "Mummy let me hold her last night!"

"And I did too!" Jared nodded. "She's called Shannon, not Julia. Mummy didn't like *Julia*."

Eden could take no more. Without warning she ran up the stairs and flung open the door to the main bedroom, angry beyond belief at the sight of her sister lying asleep with the baby snuggled on her chest. With Billy, Janet and the twins close on her heels, Eden ran to the bed, aware that Esme had woken up.

"It's time for me to take Julia home! She's *my* baby, Esme! You can't do this to me!"

She saw her sister instinctively pull the baby tighter towards her.

"Give her to me!"

"No." Esme's eyes filled with tears. "I'm sorry but I just can't do it. She's my daughter. I've given birth to her, and I've registered her as mine. She's Shannon Julia Jones."

Billy entered the room

"She's *my* daughter as well, Ez. If I have to drag this through the courts, then I will."

Janet looked from one of her daughters to the other.

"I had a terrible feeling this was going to happen. Esme, please re-consider, otherwise you're going to tear this family apart." She ushered the twins out of the door. "Boys, please go and play in your room for a little while."

James and Jared raced along the landing. Esme shook her head.

"At first I thought I could do it, but I can't. Mum, could *you* have given away one of us two?"

Eden waited for her mother's reply, which was not forthcoming. Distraught, she stared at her sister, a clawing, scratching lioness willing to kill to protect her cub. Sobs came

117

thick and fast as reality dawned there and then that she would never be a mother. She sank to her knees in despair.

"Billy! The nursery's ready! There's four bottles of baby milk made up in the fridge! What am I going to do?"

She sobbed louder and felt Billy's arms around her.

"We'll fight through the courts. Don't worry. We still have a chance."

Somewhere in the distance she heard the front door open. Footsteps. Her brother-in-law's voice boomed loud enough to wake the baby, who gave a thin, reedy cry.

"What the fuck's going on here?"

His anger made her sob louder. She felt Billy move away from her and stand up.

"Ez has decided to keep the baby. I suppose you already knew that though, didn't you?"

"No, I didn't." Aron replied forcefully. "I'll speak to Ez in a minute. Everybody out... go and wait downstairs!"

With despair, Eden slowly got to her feet and took a longing last look at her daughter.

"You've broken my heart, Esme."

With Billy beside her she held her head high and walked out onto the landing, passing by her nephews' room who giggled as they played together in their usual carefree way. Her heart felt heavy; her sister now had three children, and she, Eden, had none. Life definitely was not fair. God played with her; first He took away her womb, then He promised her a baby, and now He had taken that precious baby away. Was it a test of endurance to see how much grief she could take before she cracked? Eden felt whatever faith she might have had slip-sliding away quicker than ice in the summer heat. It was a relief to reach the front room, sink onto the settee and dissolve into tears in relative privacy.

She felt Billy pat her back.

"Don't worry. We'll sort this out. Let's wait here for a minute until Aron comes down. I *know* he's on our side."

Eden leaned against Billy and closed her eyes. Outside the birds twittered and people went about their daily business, while behind closed doors she knew that four people's lives had been irretrievably damaged beyond repair.

Chapter Twenty Nine

Aron shut the bedroom door firmly and locked it. He looked at his tear-stained wife, who sobbed and held the baby close to her chest.

"Tell me what the hell's going on! If you think I'm bringing up Billy's kid, then you've got another think coming...this was *not* in the game plan! I'm going to take the baby downstairs and give her to Ede and Billy. We've enough to feed and clothe the two we *do* have!"

"No!"

Esme's eyes were wild. Aron took a deep breath and let the anger bubble out of him. He sat down on the side of the bed and took his wife's hand in his.

"The baby is Billy's. I am not, I repeat...*not*...working my arse off to feed another man's child. If you keep Ede on your side I'm sure she'll let you see Shannon as often as you like. If you keep on denying them the chance to be parents, then we'll get stuck with a huge lawyer's bill and you'll probably never see your sister again."

Sobbing reached a zenith all around him; Esme and the baby wailed, while downstairs Eden's distress rumbled up through the floorboards. He played his trump card.

"It's me or Shannon. If you don't give the baby to Eden like you promised, then I'm out of here and you'll be on your own with three kids. I love you to the moon and back, but you can't do this to them, and I won't let you."

Gently, ignoring his wife's increased sobbing, he prised the screaming infant from her arms. He looked down at the baby, who had Esme's features, but with Billy's shock of red hair. The baby ceased crying and regarded him seriously with eyes of the same colour grey as the woman he adored. He stifled a smile.

"Little girl…let's go. Your mummy's waiting downstairs."

He made his way slowly towards the bedroom door and unlocked it. He glanced behind him. Esme's stab of hatred shot through his heart and smashed it into virtual pieces.

"Stay here. I'll be back up in a minute. You know it's the right thing to do."

There was no reply. He closed the door behind him and went downstairs.

***

The two of them sat together in their grief on the settee; he realised Janet had obviously carried on with her duties and had gone in to the boys' room. He made a mental note to apologise to his mother-in-law for his outburst of temper.

Aron met Eden's eyes. With a resolve he didn't know he had, he walked over to her.

"She's all yours, but if I were you I'd keep away for a while. I didn't realise Ez was going to take it this far. She's pretty upset, and she'll need time to get over it."

He placed the baby in Eden's arms, who promptly dissolved into a fresh bout of weeping.

"You'll probably have to change her name by deed poll. Ez registered her birth yesterday."

"Thanks so much for this, mate." Billy stood up and held out his hand. "You don't know how much it means to us."

Aron shook the proffered hand.

"Take a week off work. You'd both better get off home now. I've got to go and pacify Ez, who now thinks I'm on par with the Moors' Murderers, Fred West, and Jack the Ripper all rolled into one."

He breathed a sigh of relief as he closed the front door behind them. Janet and the boys came down the stairs.

"Shall I start dinner?" Janet enquired. "The twins are hungry, I think."

Aron nodded.

"Sure, thanks Janet. Sorry about earlier, but it had to be done."

"If you want my opinion, you did the right thing."

He was surprised at his mother-in-law's words. He crept upstairs, and noticed the bedroom door still remained closed. He turned the handle quietly, and went in. Esme lay on her side, eyes open, and stared at the wall.

"They've gone, love. It's for the best."

He sat down on the bed and took her in his arms. She made no resistance.

"I love you."

There was no reply. He was unsure which was preferable, the weeping or her silence.

Chapter Thirty

She felt euphoric to have Julia home, but was all fingers and thumbs. She remembered helping to bathe and dress the twins as toddlers, but a floppy newborn was something else. *However had her sister managed with twins*? Eden's second attempt to dress Julia in a Babygro was as unsuccessful as the first. Frustration made her break out into a sweat.

"Billy!"

She turned to look at him as he entered the nursery.

"What?"

"I can't get this growbag on Julia."

The baby began to wail for no apparent reason as far as she could tell. She moved aside to let Billy stand in front of the changing mat.

"It needs the male spatial awareness trait that you women just don't have." Billy chuckled. "Watch and learn, and by the way it's a Babygro. We're not raising a ton of tomatoes here."

Within a few moments she realised her mistake as she watched Billy lift a screaming Julia with one hand and then place the opened Babygro on the mat with the other. He then gently laid the baby back on top of it.

"See...? You can then slot the arms and legs in place. It's easier than trying to do it any other way."

Feeling stupid, Eden pushed Billy out of the way.

"I'll take over now. You can go."

As she pressed the last popper in place, the baby, red-faced and furious, lifted up her legs and filled the clean nappy. Faeces leaked out onto the Babygro, and Eden stifled the urge to retch. Pudgy limbs moved in a piston-like fashion, distributing the excreta to a wider area. She undid the Babygro, pulled flailing arms and legs back out, and took off the nappy, dropping both onto the carpet. Tiny fingers became soiled as they made contact with the changing mat. The stench was overpowering.

"Billy!"

There was no answer. She reached over to the window and opened it. Billy, headphones on ears, lay supine on a sun lounger.

"Billy! I've got a Code Brown!"

Julia, naked, protested loudly. Eden, flustered, cleaned the baby's hands with a wipe, then lifted two little legs with one hand and wiped up the mess as best she could. However, it was clear to her that her daughter now desperately needed a bath. Sweaty with effort, she took a clean towel from a drawer in the changing table, and holding Julia in the crook of one elbow went into the bathroom.

She had not used the small bath before. She put Julia down onto a towel, then filled the baby bath with a few inches of water and added some drops of Infacare soap. Lusty screams reached fever pitch. Eden stooped over the bath and lifted Julia into the warm water. The baby calmed down somewhat, but immediately felt as slippery as an eel. Hot, bothered and panicky, Eden grabbed the top of a little arm and rinsed her daughter's hair and body as quickly as she could.

Unused to stooping, she was glad to lift the baby out and straighten up to ease a slight backache. The screaming had petered out, and she could see that Julia seemed to enjoy being wrapped snugly in a towel. All too soon she realised that she had forgotten to bring a clean nappy from the nursery. By the time she got back to the changing mat, a little patch of urine had found its way onto the towel.

Eden, tired from the previous night's lack of sleep, felt tears sting her eyes. *She needed her mother's advice, but of course Esme needed her help more at the moment.*

She dressed Julia in a clean nappy and Babygro, then took her downstairs to where Billy still lay listening to music. She gently prodded one finger into his ribs. Billy opened his eyes and took off his headphones.

"I called you for help with a Code Brown."

"Oh." He yawned. "I didn't hear you. You told me to go away, so I did."

"I want to sit here for a bit. I'm tired. Would you mind clearing up? There's a bit of a mess upstairs."

Reluctantly, Billy stood up. With one hand Eden dragged a sun lounger into the shade and lay down, placing the baby on her chest as Esme had done. She felt exhausted, but pleased that Julia's crying had ceased. A plane flew overhead, and birds sang their usual song. She tried to relax but was unable to sleep; thoughts of her mother-in-law's dead baby swam behind her eyes. *She was a mother herself now, and she must be forever watchful.*

Chapter Thirty One

Now she knew why cows bellowed for days on end when their calves were taken away to be sold. She felt utterly bereft and unable to function. When her milk came in on the third day, her breasts were uncomfortably sore and engorged. Esme took to her bed and wallowed in grief, too wrapped up in her misery to bother answering a tentative knock on the door.

"Mummy?"

She wiped her eyes and sat up. Jared's head popped around the door.

"Can I have a cuddle, please?"

She nodded through her tears. Jared ran towards the bed and with one leap landed against her. Esme masked the pain in her breasts and held him in a tight embrace.

"Don't cry anymore, Mummy. James is watching Cee Beebies, but I've drawn you a picture downstairs."

Her son's words caused another river of tears to flow.

"Th-That's nice..." She sniffed. "And show it to Daddy as well, when he comes home from work."

Her head and eyelids felt heavy, but she managed a thin smile as her mother came in carrying a cup.

"I've made you some tea. Come down and sit with us, eh? The twins are missing you."

"Thanks." She took the cup and left her other arm around Jared. "I will in a minute, after the midwife has been. Mum... I don't know what I'd have done without you."

Tears welled up and splashed down her cheeks. The doorbell rang, and Janet Prentice waved away her remark.

"I'm just happy to be able to help. I'll send Denise up. Jared ... come downstairs now."

***

"How are you doing, Mrs Jones?"

Esme broke into a fresh wave of tears.

"My breasts are so sore! I physically ache to feed my baby!"

Denise nodded.

"If you visit your GP, they can prescribe some medication to help. In the meantime use cooled cabbage leaves on the breasts for about thirty minutes, and drink sage or peppermint tea. I'll examine you, and then I'll go and check on the baby if you give me your sister's address. How are you coping mentally?"

"It's awful." Esme sobbed. "I never imagined in my wildest nightmares that I'd feel this way. I thought I could just hand Shannon over to my sister and be done with it."

Denise opened a capacious bag.

"There's nothing stronger than the mother and baby bond. It'll take time to get over it, but again your GP can help if you're really struggling."

"No, I don't want to become hooked on anti-depressants." Esme sighed and shook her head. "That's a definite no-no for me."

Denise took out a notebook and pen from the bag.

"Then focus on the children who *are* in your care and give them lots of love. What about a counsellor maybe? Would you like me to refer you for counselling to the Mindfulness Centre at Moreton Hall?"

"Yes, okay." Esme wiped her eyes. "I think I need some sort of support. It's going to be hard for me to get over this. I can't lock myself away forever."

"Good." Denise smiled at her. "I'll send off the referral tomorrow."

***

James continued to stare at the TV as she entered the room, but she smiled at her more sensitive son who jumped up and ran towards her.

"Mummy!" Jared grinned at her. "Do you feel better now?"

She hugged him.

"A bit." She lied. "I wanted to come down and see my boys."

"Do you want to see my picture?"

She sat down heavily on the settee and tried to remember what day it was.

"Of course. Run and get it. If it's a good one, I'll put it on the wall.

The tinny American accents on the TV cartoon programme irritated her. Esme reached for the remote control and turned down the volume.

"Mum!" James looked at her in irritation.

"You can still hear it. I've got a headache."

Jared returned and held out a piece of paper.

"It's all of us, Mummy."

She took the drawing and looked with despair at Aron, her sons, and herself holding a baby. Her arms felt empty. She wondered briefly how Eden was getting on.

Chapter Thirty Two

It had been a busy few days, but he had managed. Aron looked up with disappointment as Billy drove into the yard on the first day in August. Heat radiated off the top of the caravan, and sweat poured through his overalls already at only nine o'clock. He got up to switch the kettle on, ensuring his back would be the first thing Billy saw.

"Mornin'!"

Aron lifted a spoon in greeting as he added coffee to two cups, but did not turn around.

"How's it going?"

"No sleep, but hey, you know how it is. Eden's not finding it easy, but then again how many new mothers do?"

Aron nodded and waited for the kettle to boil, listening with annoyance as Billy settled himself at his desk and hummed a tune.

"I'm not getting much sleep either. Ez is crying all night."

The humming stopped abruptly.

"Sorry mate, I mean, er... "

"Forget it." Aron added two spoonfuls of sugar to Billy's coffee. "What the fuck's it got to do with me, eh?"

He put the cup down on Billy's desk a little more forcibly than usual.

"Cheers." Billy gave a nod of thanks. "Ede can bring Julia over to see Ez any time she wants."

Aron shook his head.

"That's not a good idea. Her milk's in and the kid's crying'll set it off. I remember that from last time. Tell her to leave it about twenty years."

Billy's very presence began to grate on his nerves. Aron stood up as a laden tow truck reversed in.

"Christ, I'm glad I wasn't driving *that* one."

He took a gulp of coffee and then went out into the yard. The heat-laden air was preferable to a palpable tension in the office.

***

It had got to the point where he dreaded coming home. He had always prided himself on being one of life's fixers; practical with a spanner or handy with a shoulder to cry on. However, Esme's grief was beyond his capabilities; raw, unending misery greeted him night after night with the result that both boys now turned to him to solve childish problems, puzzled at their mother's sudden disinterest. Janet did the best she could but it wasn't enough; his wife wanted the one thing that she could never have.

Aron turned his key in the lock, and two mini tornadoes threw themselves at him.

"Daddy!" James and Jared shouted in eerie unison.

Janet Prentice appeared in the hallway. She smiled and wiped her hands on her apron.

"Hello Aron. Good day?"

He shrugged, put his arms around both boys and kissed the top of their heads."

"Have you been good for Mummy and Nanny?"

"Yes!" They chanted together. "Nanny's made a chicken pie!"

He looked up at Janet.

"How's she been today?"

"Ah, so-so." Janet replied with a grimace. "She's sitting in the garden. Hopefully the first counselling appointment will arrive in the next week or so. I think she needs it. I'm going to head off to see Eden now you're here. I seem to be very popular at the moment."

Aron nodded.

"Thanks for all you're doing. I really appreciate it."

Janet waved away his remark.

"I'll come back every day until she's feeling better. I'll try and get her and the boys out to the park tomorrow, somehow everything seems better when you're outside, doesn't it? Dinner's all ready to be dished up, by the way."

"Cheers, Janet." Aron nodded. "See you tomorrow."

***

The boys ran ahead of him to the garden and raced each other to the top of the climbing frame. Esme watched them sightlessly, her mind elsewhere. Aron sat down beside her.

"Hey, babe, your mum's got dinner ready. Do you want to dish it up or shall I?"

There was no immediate response. Aron sighed and kissed her cheek.

"Earth to Esme… the kids are hungry."

She turned towards him.

"I'll do it."

Her voice was a flat monotone. He watched her move robotically from the sun lounger to the kitchen, then returned Jared's wave and followed her inside. As she sliced the pie into segments he came and stood behind her and put his arms around her waist.

"Love you."

She put down the knife, turned to face him, and buried her face in his shoulder.

"I'm so sorry!" She sobbed. "I can't seem to think straight!"

He wiped her tears with his fingers and held her tight.

"We'll get through this. The boys need you, and I need you. We're still a family. It's early days yet. Let's just take it one day at a time."

She nodded.

"I never thought I'd feel this way."

"I know." He kissed her. "I know it's hard for you. Hang in there. It'll get better."

His voice had an optimistic tone that in reality he did not feel. In fact, he dreaded the coming of every evening after the boys had gone to bed, because then he was alone with her sorrow.

Chapter Thirty Three

Eden smiled at her mother standing on the doorstep. She had never been so pleased to see anybody in her entire life.

"I'm so glad you're here! She won't stop crying!"

She felt like howling herself, but needed to show her mother that she was able to cope. In reality she felt lost, out of her depth, and totally clueless. She also had a nasty suspicion that Julia needed her real mother, and that real mother was not *her*.

"All babies cry." Janet Prentice stepped into the hallway. "Did you think you were going to get one that slept for four hours in-between feeds until it went to school?"

Eden closed the door and ran a hand through her hair. The baby's wailing had reached fever pitch, and she had a stress headache.

"No, of course not, but surely it's not right that she cries so much? She's not long had a bottle, so she can't be hungry. She doesn't sleep a lot at night either, and she's often sick."

She followed her mother into the front room, where Julia, furious and red-faced, pummeled the air with tiny fists. Janet scooped up the baby from her Moses basket and rocked the little body to and fro in her arms.

"See how her legs are drawn up? She's probably got colic. Some babies are unlucky like that. Ez had it and the doctor gave me Merbentyl syrup for her, but I'm not sure if they still give it to newborns. You'll have to go to the surgery and find out. If not, try winding her for longer. Sometimes they're so hungry that they gulp down too much air with the milk and it gives them gut ache. Before we got that syrup your father gave her a few drops of whisky in her milk."

"No way!" Eden looked at her mother in surprise.

"Yep." Janet nodded. "I never realised he'd done it until we woke up one morning after having slept all night. I thought Esme was dead ... I sent him into her room to find out. He woke her up and she started screaming all over again."

"Probably had a hangover!" Eden remarked drily, as another flash of dead baby raced through her brain.

Janet chuckled, hiked the baby up onto her shoulder and gently but expertly tapped her back until Julia gave a loud belch. Eden felt a stab of jealousy as Julia's screaming decreased. She herself wanted to be soothed in her mother's arms once more just for a moment, to ease her fraught nerves and relinquish the agonising responsibility of keeping a tiny creature alive that did not seem to like her at all.

To her acute annoyance the baby's eyelids closed. She sat down on the settee next to her mother and held out her arms for the infant.

"Can I hold her please, Mum? She hardly ever sleeps in my arms like that."

"Wait a minute until she's properly asleep." Janet looked down benignly at the baby. "This brings back memories. Funny how one day it's your child and the next your grandchild. Where does all the time go?"

Eden could wait no longer. She carefully lifted Julia into her arms, still warm from her mother's embrace and now smelling faintly of her mother's perfume instead of her own. To her intense annoyance the baby's eyes pinged open, accompanied by a yelp of discontent.

"She hates me, Mum! I've taken her away from Ez!"

Janet shook her head.

"Don't be silly. You're imagining things that simply aren't true. The more uptight you get, the more she'll scream. Try and relax a bit and give her lots of cuddles."

She rocked Julia back and forth as she had seen her mother do. The baby settled into a fitful sleep, and Eden asked the one question that she could not put off any longer.

"How's Ez doing?"

"Not too good, but it's early days." Janet replied. "She's been referred for counselling, as she doesn't want anti-depressants."

"Oh God!" Eden fought the urge to cry. "What have I done to her? What have I done to this baby? I've taken her away from her mother!"

A few tears slid down her cheeks, and she reached over to take a tissue from the coffee table.

"Now now, I don't want to hear any of that." Janet replied in a firm tone. "It was *her* choice to have the baby for you in the first place. You've both got some adjusting to do, but the two of you will get there in the end."

Eden blew her nose.

"I can't begin to even *know* what Ez is going through. Do you think it's a good idea if I visit her with Julia?"

"I wouldn't at the moment." Janet shook her head. "She's still grieving. Plus the fact her milk's in, which makes it ten times worse. Julia's crying will stimulate it to flow."

Fresh tears fell onto Julia's cardigan, which she had knitted so carefully. Eden sighed.

"Oh God! Sometimes I wish I'd never agreed to this!"

Janet, practical as ever, gave a *tut* of annoyance.

"Well, you can hardly send her back where she came from! You will have to *learn* to be a parent, just the same as we all did."

"How am I going to do that if you're always helping Esme?" Eden replied petulantly.

"I'm *here* aren't I?" Janet gave Eden an unforgiving stare. "Dad doesn't retire until next year, and I go to the one who needs me the most. Lately it's been Esme, but now she's recovering a bit more I can help *you*, so don't go giving me the guilt trip."

"Sorry."

The baby woke up and opened its mouth to scream. Eden sighed.

"Why won't she stop crying?"

Janet stroked Julia's fingers.

"Babies can also pick up on any stress and discontent around them. If you're relaxed, then they're calmer. Try to chill a bit if you can."

"How can I?" Eden wailed. "I've made everybody so unhappy!"

Chapter Thirty Four

Esme undid her seat belt and looked across to Aron.

"Will Billy mind that you've taken time off this morning? I could have waited until I'm allowed to drive again in a couple more weeks."

"No, it's best that you see someone as soon as possible." Aron replied. "Billy can hold the fort until I get back."

Esme nodded, climbed out of the car and walked nervously into the Mindfulness Centre, giving her name at the reception desk. She was directed upstairs and tapped nervously on the consulting room door marked *M. McKinnon, Counsellor*.

"Come in!"

She came face-to-face with a middle-aged lady, rather portly, who sported short, closely cropped salt-and-pepper hair. A crisp white blouse peeked out from underneath a tailored grey suit.

"I'm Marcia, and you must be Esme. Do come and sit down. There's some water on the table if you wish."

Esme closed the door and sat down in a comfortable armchair opposite the counsellor.

"Thanks. Hi Marcia, Denise Parry referred me."

"Yes, I have your notes here." Marcia nodded. "An interesting situation you find yourself in. Would you like to tell me a bit more? I'm allowed twenty minutes for all my NHS referrals, as there are so many patients I need to see."

Esme crossed her legs and clung onto a tissue in her right hand.

"That's all right. In a nutshell, my sister is barren and I offered to have a baby for her. I'd already completed my family and thought I could do it. The baby, a girl I called Shannon, was born on the twenty second of July, but I found I didn't want to give her up. I've been having a hard time coming to terms with the fact that my sister is now Shannon's mother."

Marcia scribbled down a few notes before looking up.

"And what have your feelings been towards your sister since the baby's been born?"

Esme took in a shaky breath.

"I'm jealous of her happiness, while I've been left feeling so miserable. Eden's got my daughter and I want her back, and I'm also angry, angry as hell at my own stupidity for thinking I could do this."

"I see." Marcia took a sip of water. "Have you seen your sister to tell her about your feelings?"

Esme slowly shook her head.

"Not yet. I've heard from my mother and husband... he works with my brother-in-law, that motherhood isn't coming naturally to my sister, but at least she's got the baby she always wanted."

"How about your other children?" Marcia asked gently. "How do *they* feel about the baby?"

"I've got twin boys. They wanted to keep her, but eight year old kids are adaptable. They seem to be getting over it. My arms are empty, it's unbearable." She closed her eyes briefly against threatening tears before carrying on. "I'm walking around in a daze."

She was glad to see Marcia nodding in sympathy.

"Do you think in time you'd like to meet up with your sister and see how the baby is getting on?"

Esme shrugged.

"Of course I'd like to see my daughter, but my instinct would be to take her home."

"How about just meeting with your sister without the baby?" Marcia replied.

"Hmm, that's feasible." Esme nodded. "It might help to talk to her alone. All this has caused a bit of a rift between us. I feel guilty for shutting her out at the birth. She should have been there but I couldn't bear to hand Shannon over."

"It'll be a good start." Marcia replied, "And probably better if you also meet on neutral ground, say a local park or somewhere like that."

Esme sighed.

"I'll certainly try, although I'm not ready just yet. There's a little playpark along Newmarket High Street. The boys can play there, or there's Christchurch Park nearer Eden and Billy. Mum will be able to look after Shannon. No... I'll have to get used to calling her *Julia*, or the poor child will get confused."

Marcia nodded in sympathy.

"Emotions run high when we're getting over a birth, let alone adding in *your* personal circumstances. Wait until you're ready, and then try and make contact with your sister. Come back and tell me how you get on."

"Thanks." Esme gave Marcia a thin smile. "I will."

Marcia jotted down a few more notes.

"And your husband...is he supportive?"

"He does his best, but he's happy not having another mouth to feed." Esme replied with a sigh. "I think he's found it hard to cope with my low mood recently though. He's waiting for me to snap out of it, I think. Men don't really understand the emotions involved in carrying a baby and giving birth to it, do they?"

"Of course not." Marcia laughed. "If they had babies, I expect the birth rate would be much lower. Don't forget to explain all your conflicting thoughts to your husband. Talking together is the best way to move forward."

Esme stood up.

"I know you're right. I'd better go... he's waiting in the car for me and has to get back to work. I hadn't thought of meeting Eden alone, and so thanks for that."

"My pleasure." Marcia got to her feet. "I can give you three more appointments, so please make another one at the desk before you go."

***

"Have the boys been good?"

Esme stood at the back door and listened to squeals of delight as her sons chased each other around the garden with water pistols. Janet Prentice nodded from the depths of the sun lounger.

"Of course they have! What did she say?"

Esme waved to the boys and sat down on a nearby bench.

"She wants me to meet up with Eden alone, so you'll have to look after the baby if Billy's at work. I need to leave it a while though, because I'm still a bit sore to go walking around outside, and plus the fact I don't really know what to say to her."

"Don't leave it too long." Janet sat up straighter. "You two need to sort things out. I don't want my family ripped apart."

Esme looked at her mother.

"How's she managing?"

"She'll get there." Janet replied. "It's all new to her at the moment and she needs to gain some confidence."

"That's why it's *doubly* hard for me." Esme said wearily. "I *know* I could do a better job, and it breaks my heart to think that my little girl isn't getting the best care."

Janet shook her head.

"I'd step in if I thought Julia wasn't being looked after properly. Eden's a bit highly strung, that's all, but the baby is okay, a bit sicky, but okay."

A wave of disappointment washed over Esme. Her mother's reply was not the one she had hoped to hear.

***

Aron, hands in soapsuds, passed her another plate.

"Was it worth going?"

Esme picked up a tea towel and shrugged.

"She suggested that Ede and I meet up without the baby. I hadn't thought of that, but counsellors never really say anything one way or the other … they let *you* do the talking, don't they?"

"I don't know." Aron placed a dripping cup on the draining board. "I've never been to one."

Eden dried the plate and put it in a nearby cupboard.

"Neither had I before, but I realise that however many times I go, it's not going to bring the baby back. I'll give it one more go but after that I don't think I'll bother anymore."

"No, it won't bring her back." Aron scraped the bottom of a saucepan with a wire pad. "But hopefully you'll get something out of it?"

Esme shrugged, then picked up the cup and dried it.

"She also said *we* had to talk more."

Aron turned to look at her.

"Well…we *are* talking, aren't we?"

"Not about washing up or boys' homework. We have to talk about our feelings regarding the baby."

"You already know how I feel." Aron rinsed the saucepan and put it on the draining board. "It belongs to Ede and Billy. Why should I be saddled with thousands of quid over twenty years to bring it up?"

"It's a *she*, Aron." Esme sighed. "I'm trying real hard not to bring the whole family down with my misery, but it's something you'll never understand unless you've carried a baby in your womb and given birth to it."

Aron yawned.

"I haven't got a womb. I'm a bloke. Why the hell did you agree to do it in the first place then?"

It was a question she had asked herself hundreds of times already. Esme picked up the saucepan.

"Because I wanted to make Eden happy."

"You wanted to be a heroine and be remembered forever, more like." Aron chuckled.

His words hit home like a thunderbolt.

"Who knows?" She replied. "Is that *bad*?"

"Only if it makes you unhappy, and it obviously has." Aron pulled the plug out of the sink. "In all the years we've been married I've never seen you so depressed. As far as I can tell, being a heroine ain't doing a great deal for you, or for this whole family come to that."

With typical male logic he had winkled out a reason that even she, Esme, had not even thought of. *Did she really go through it all just for acclaim?* Esme put the saucepan away, hung up her tea towel, and considered whether Aron just viewed her as a truly miserable, self-obsessed bitch.

Chapter Thirty Five

"Do sit down. It's nice to see you again."

Esme sat down in the same squashy armchair.

"Hello Marcia. I thought I'd come back again and chat about something my husband Aron said."

Marcia McKinnon nodded and opened her file of notes.

"So you've been talking then?"

Esme smiled.

"Er...yeah, but I didn't like what I heard. Aron's opinion was that I might have had the baby because I wanted to be a heroine and be remembered forever."

"Well, it's human nature to want to be remembered fondly in some way."

Esme took a sip of water.

"Yes, but is that why I had the baby?"

Marcia skimmed through the first few pages of her notebook and then looked across the table.

"When you were a child, did you receive praise and encouragement from your parents for school work and hobbies for instance?"

"They drove us to loads of after-school clubs and activities, but I remember hating to talk over what had gone on every time we got home. Eden went to different clubs as she was older than me. Mum would ask us what we'd been doing and Eden would burble on, but I'd just say I had a good time. Dad wasn't much of a talker, but he was the one we always went to in a crisis."

Marcia chuckled.

"So your childhood was happy?"

"Oh yes. My parents weren't particularly demonstrative, but we knew we were loved."

"Did you yearn to be hugged and kissed by your parents?"

Esme thought for a moment while she heard the clock tick away precious minutes.

"Not... really... I suppose I grew up just like *them*. We're not the touchy-feely type."

Esme was not keen on baring her soul, but waited with interest for Marcia's next question. The counsellor shuffled her papers and then continued.

"Were you close to your sister?"

Esme shook her head.

"She was five years older. Of course I looked up to her as a little sister would do, but she was off with her friends and always seemed so grown up. Maybe she looked upon me as an irritation... I don't know. Five years is an unbridgeable chasm when you're a kid. She was going out with boys at sixteen, and I was still playing with dolls."

"Yes, that's true enough." Marcia replied with a nod. "But you've grown closer in recent years?"

"Only after we'd both got married and settled down. She studied English at university, so I hardly saw her when I was a teenager. I suppose what you're trying to get at is whether I had the baby for her to make her notice her little sister? There could be something in that I suppose, but I'd never really considered any of this until Aron mentioned it. I think mostly all I wanted to do in the first place was to make her happy. I don't think I really ever considered my own feelings."

"And you *have* made her happy, I'm sure." Marcia replied with a smile. "What you've done for her is a wonderful thing.

Now you can sit back and enjoy the fact that you've given your sister a family."

"But I *can't* sit back, that's the trouble." Esme sighed. "That baby is *mine*. I want her back."

Marcia drank some water.

"But think how upset you would make your sister if you took that baby away. You would rock the boat, so to speak. Also, you said last time that your husband doesn't want another mouth to feed. The status quo as it is seems agreeable to both your sister and your husband."

"But not to *me*." Esme shook her head. "Not to me."

Marcia put down her glass and sat back in her chair.

"I don't know if you're aware of this, but in other countries, for example America, surrogates have different rights to what they have over here. In the USA your sister would be automatically considered as the baby's mother right from the start."

Esme looked at Marcia in surprise.

"Really? Thank goodness the UK is a bit soft! Look, I'd better be getting along. I know time's running away and that you've got another patient waiting. I will make a real effort to try and get over this, but it's so *hard*. Every fibre of my being is reaching out to that baby."

"Give it time." Marcia replied gently. "And don't forget you can have another appointment with me if you think you might need one."

Esme made her way out to the car and flopped down into the driver's seat. As far as she was concerned, any further visits to a counsellor would be a complete waste of everyone's time.

Chapter Thirty Six

A few early autumn leaves blew across her path as Esme walked through Christchurch Park to the Mansion Tea Room. There were four hours which she had deliberately not filled before she needed to pick the boys up from school. Her empty stomach grumbled, and she knew she was at least fifteen minutes early for the meeting.

As she approached the low brick building she could see that her sister had arrived even earlier. Eden sat on one of the iron patio chairs and stirred her tea in a desultory fashion. Esme pulled her jacket around her against a sudden chilly breeze, and with a pounding heart walked up to her sister's table.

"Hi."

Eden, startled, banged her spoon against the side of her cup.

"Oh, sorry, I was miles away!"

Esme thought her sister had lost some weight. She took in the black rings under Eden's eyes, and an overall impression of sadness.

"I'll just go inside and get some coffee and something to eat."

Inside, the café was empty. Esme, mouth still dry with nerves at the sight of her sister, ordered beans on toast and an expresso. She wandered back out to the patio, where Eden still sat lost in thought.

"They'll bring it out in a minute."

She took a seat and scrambled her brain for something else to say.

"Thanks for agreeing to meet up."

She was unprepared to see her sister's body suddenly wracked with sobs. Eden avoided her gaze, wiped her eyes, and stared at her cup.

"I'm sorry for causing you so much misery!"

Esme felt tears sting the back of her own eyes, but decided to keep her resolve not to break down. Indeed, she had already shed enough tears for a river. She drew in a shaky breath as her fingers sought Eden's hand across the table.

"It was my idea to go through with it in the first place. I'm sorry too, that you weren't at the birth. It was completely selfish of me." She swallowed a lump in her throat. "How's Julia?"

"I – I don't think I'm a very good mother." Eden sobbed. "She cries a lot. Mum says she's got colic. I took her to the GP, but he didn't really want to give her anything."

The waitress appeared with a laden tray, and stood there awkwardly.

"Beans on toast and an expresso?"

"Thanks." Esme held up one hand. "That's me."

She was famished. She let Eden's crying cease while she ate. Presently she took a gulp of coffee and smiled at her sister.

"Have you tried putting her on your lap and massaging her back?"

"No." Eden shook her head. "I don't really know what to do. Billy says all babies cry, but he's at work all day and I have to listen to it."

"There's also Gripe Water that you can get from the chemist."

"Thanks." Eden gave a thin smile. "I'll take any advice I can get."

"When she starts on solids at about four months, then the colic will improve." Esme finished her coffee. "James was a bit colicky as I remember."

"I've brought some photos for you." Eden fished in her bag. "If you'd like them?"

Sooner or later she knew the day would come when she would need to set eyes on her daughter. Esme steeled herself and took the booklet with shaking hands.

"Thanks."

Two month old Shannon asleep, Shannon awake, Shannon lying in Billy's arms, and Shannon being fed by her smiling sister. She would miss her daughter's first smile, her first steps, and her first day at school. Esme swallowed against rising bile in the back of her throat and took a deep breath.

"They're lovely."

Apart from Billy's red hair, the proof that Shannon was her daughter stared at her starkly in the harsh light of day; the same grey eyes, facial features and oval shape of head. *There was nothing of Eden about her at all.*

"She's the image of you, Ez." Eden wiped her eyes and sniffed.

Eden knew it as well. Esme nodded, too wrapped up in the images of her daughter to speak straight away. The baby's eyes looked into her soul, pleading for its mother.

"She's adorable."

She closed the booklet, lest her heart become broken all over again. Her eyes felt watery, and she blinked.

"Shall we have a walk? Or do you have to get back?"

"Mum's got Julia, and she doesn't mind how long I'm out." Eden stood up. "Yes, let's have a stroll around the park."

148

The September sun had rose a little higher in the sky. Esme slung her bag over one shoulder and followed her sister out of the café. It was strange to be in close proximity to Eden again, and she noticed a pronounced weight loss as her sister stood up.

"Are you okay?" Esme enquired as they walked. "You seem thinner than I remember."

From her peripheral vision she was aware of Eden's stare.

"You mean has the cancer come back?"

"No, no. I didn't mean that at all." Esme shook her head. "It's just that you're a lot slimmer around the middle."

"Thanks. I'll take that as a compliment then." Eden chuckled. "I'm so busy with Julia that sometimes I forget to eat."

A stab of jealousy shot through Esme's body.

"You can't let kids take over your whole life."

"She's a bit of a handful at the moment." Eden replied quietly. "I feed her, wind her and change her nappy. Then sometimes after all that she's sick and I have to give her another feed. She doesn't sleep a lot either. Some days I'm on the go for hours until Billy comes home to help. Mum's been helping of course, but she does have her own life to live and she also needs to help *you*. Billy's mother wants to interfere, but we've never got on much, so I haven't encouraged her."

A woman and her toddler daughter threw bread to a few ducks meandering around the lake. Esme looked away and focused her attention on Eden.

"It'll get better, I can assure you. Mum doesn't need to help me so much now anyway. By the way, if she's sick a lot, she may be intolerant to a cow's milk formula. Try the SMA Wysoy brand and see if that settles her more. Mum probably didn't know that, as I don't think it was around when we were babies."

"Thanks. The health visitor suggested that as well. I'll definitely give it a go.. I...I feel guilty for what I've done to you though." Eden sighed. "I've taken away your baby. I can't sleep at night thinking about you and how we used to be."

Esme replied with a lightness of tone that she did not really feel.

"It was *I* who suggested it, and I'm glad you have the family you always wanted."

Eden nodded.

"I – I wanted to ask you something."

"Oh?" Esme looked at her sister with interest.

"Yeah...Billy's cousin Tom is getting married on October the twelfth, and we're invited. They don't want any children there. Would you like to have Julia for the day while we're at the wedding? We'll be home probably about nine that evening."

"Of course. I'd love to have her."

"That's great. I never wanted us to be estranged. Julia needs to get to know her cousins."

Esme smiled and considered that all her Christmases might have arrived at once. Shannon would be coming home briefly on October 12th, and she would have much to prepare.

Chapter Thirty Seven

She could hear Julia crying before she had even turned her key in the lock. She let herself in quietly and made her way to the front room, where her mother paced the room with the baby over her shoulder. Eden felt the now familiar tensing of her muscles and the start of another stress headache.

"How's she been?"

"Fractious." Janet Prentice replied with a sigh. "I think she's tired, but she won't give in."

"Thanks for looking after her."

Janet turned around at the end of the room and paced back towards the door.

"How'd it go with Ez?"

"Better than I expected." Eden smiled at her mother. "At least she's talking to me now. I gave her some photos."

"Good."

She reached out and took the baby. Motherhood was not working out quite as wonderful as she'd first thought. Julia's cries assaulted her ears after the relative peace of Christchurch Park, and she felt inept and clueless as to what to do to pacify her daughter. She frowned; her tension headache started up a thudding in her head.

"You go now, Mum, if you like."

"Well... I do have things to do at home." Janet reached for her bag. "Are you okay?"

She wanted to throw herself at her mother and weep for England, and Ireland, Scotland and Wales too for that matter.

"I'm absolutely fine." Eden replied with a nod. "I'm sure she'll go to sleep in a minute."

"She's not long had a bottle and a nappy change. If I were you I'd take her out in the pram and see if she'll settle."

With dismay she watched her mother walk away, and then closed the front door and carried her screaming infant to the kitchen. While she waited for the kettle to boil she jiggled Julia up and down.

"Shh!" She kissed the top of the little warm forehead. "Shh!"

When she brought a welcome cup of tea to her lips, the baby vomited across her chest and onto the floor, and then stayed mercifully silent. Eden, horrified and now covered in a layer of baby sick, stood holding a dripping Julia.

"Oh God, help me!"

She banged her cup down forcefully on the kitchen table and ran upstairs. She laid the baby down on the bathroom changing mat, which caused Julia's mouth to open wide in protest. She filled the bath and added some Infacare, then took off Julia's and her own sodden clothes and put them in the laundry basket. She wiped down the changing mat, then keeping a tight hold of her daughter she stepped gingerly into the bath.

The telephone's shrill ring competed with Julia's cries. Eden, with one arm supporting the baby, washed herself and Julia as best she could. Then still clutching her furious bundle, she manoeuvered herself out of the bath and onto a clean towel. She wrapped the baby in a pink Winnie-the-Pooh bathrobe and put her back down on the changing mat while she got herself dressed. The telephone rang again just as a squirt of excreta stained the bathrobe.

Eden began to cry, long heaving sobs which joined in with Julia's high pitched wail. With tears streaming down her face she divested the baby of the faeces-stained robe and placed her hands under Julia's armpits to lift her into the still-warm bath water.

"Your mother has the right milk, but I can't ask her to give it to you!"

She sobbed and rinsed the baby's undercarriage again, and was determined to discover whether Julia might prefer a non-cow soya based formula milk.

***

"I phoned you earlier on. Did you go out?"

She stopped moving the baby's chair up and down with her foot, and swallowed a forkful of mash.

"Julia exploded at both ends. I had a Code Brown while having to be Queen Sick at the same time. The washing machine was on all the afternoon. What did you want?"

"Oh, poor kid!" Billy reached down to touch the baby's fingers with his own. "She's sick a lot, isn't she? I only phoned to see how you got on with Ez this morning."

Eden nodded.

"Not too bad, a bit awkward at first though. Ez says to try a soya based milk. Mum never mentioned it, but it might be that she doesn't know. If you babysit, I'll nip out to the supermarket after dinner and get some. It's easier if I go without Julia."

"Okay." Billy shrugged. "But all babies throw up and cry, don't they?"

Eden resumed gently tapping the bottom of the baby's chair.

"Yes, but Julia seems particularly good at it. If she settles better on the soya formula, then I'll keep her on that."

She chewed a mouthful of fish pie and looked down; Julia had dozed off in the chair. Eden drew in a deep breath of relief.

Chapter Thirty Eight

Aron chuckled as Billy's mouth opened into a wide yawn.

"Baby still not sleeping?"

"Not so you'd notice." Billy shuffled a few papers on his desk. "We're having a bit more success with the soya milk though, she's not throwing up as much. How long does this phase last?"

"About fourteen years, then you can't get the buggers out of bed so I've been told."

"Shit." Billy rubbed his eyes. "We've got Tom and Carol's wedding coming up tomorrow. I'll probably fall asleep in the church."

"Go home after and have a kip." Aron grinned. "Instead of all day we'll have the baby overnight as well. I'm sure Ez will jump at the chance."

"You sure?" Billy looked over at Aron in surprise.

"Yeah. Take me up on the offer before I change my mind."

Billy raised his cup of coffee.

"Cheers. Ta very much. We could use the sleep. Ede's strung out enough to snap because Julia's not putting on much weight. Will you still open up the yard tomorrow?"

"Just for the morning." Aron nodded. "Ez will enjoy being with the kids."

***

He was surprised to see Janet and Barry supervising the boys' lunches when he returned home from the yard just after noon the following day.

"Hi. Where's Ez?"

"Hello Daddy!" James and Jared shouted in eerie unison. "We've got fishfingers and chips!"

Janet looked up from buttering bread.

"She took the baby for a walk in the pram to try and get her off to sleep."

Aron shook his head.

"Her car's gone."

"Oh, we hadn't noticed." Barry shrugged. "These two little terrors have kept us busy."

He pulled his phone from the top pocket of his overalls and tapped in the number he knew off by heart. A robotic voice informed him that the number was currently unavailable and to try again later.

All through lunch and into the afternoon he had an uneasy feeling that something was not quite right. Janet and Barry went off to do some shopping, and any further calls to Esme were fruitless. The boys, unconcerned, played football in the local park whilst he sat on a bench and pretended to watch them; in reality staring hard at any woman pushing a pram that came into view.

By 5:15pm he knew there would be only one more hour of daylight, and he had started having to fend off the boys' questions. Aron made a simple meal of jacket potatoes with baked beans and sausages, and as the boys ate he tried Esme's phone again, but without success. He wolfed down his dinner and the boys' leftovers, then bathed them and absent-mindedly read both of them a story. As they watched a video for the last half an hour before bedtime, he picked up his mobile and dialled his mother-in-law's number.

"Janet? It's Aron."

"Hello." Janet's voice came down the line. "Is anything wrong?"

Aron kept his voice non-committal.

"Is Ez with you by any chance?"

"No, she isn't. Has she not been home since this morning?"

Janet sounded immediately anxious, in fact as anxious as he already was.

"I've not seen her, no." Aron sighed. "She took the car as you know, and so could be anywhere."

There was a slight hesitation on the other end of the line before he heard Janet speak again.

"Do you think something might have happened to her? Could she have gone to *your* mother?"

"I don't know, is the answer to both of those questions." Aron stated firmly. "I'll phone Mum and ask her, and then if no luck I think I'd better get in touch with the police and report her missing."

"Oh God!" Janet's voice rose in alarm. "Did she take any stuff for the baby?"

"I haven't looked, to be honest." Aron replied. "I'm not sure where to check."

"The fridge." Janet answered straight away. "Did she take the bottles that Eden brought round?"

He made his way quickly to the kitchen and opened the fridge door.

"There's six bottles in here."

"Then no, she didn't." Janet exhaled forcefully. "Can you see Eden's changing bag with the smiley faces on? It was in the hallway the last time I saw it."

He ran out of the kitchen towards the front door.

"No, that's gone."

"Ah well, at least she took some nappies and clean clothes."

Janet's words did not bring him any comfort.

"I'll make a few phone calls. If nobody has seen her, could you come and sit with the boys, please? I'll let you know, but if she's not with any friends or family then I'll need to nip down to the police station."

"Of course." Janet replied. "I'll come round anyway. I was only watching TV."

He ended the call and phoned the number he knew off by heart, while all the time wondering what the hell had happened to his wife.

"Hello."

The sound of his mother's voice was still somehow comforting.

"Mum, has Ez been round to see you today?"

"No, I haven't seen her. Why? What's the matter?"

His mother sounded as worried as he felt. Aron looked around for his car keys.

"She hasn't come home from an outing to walk the baby this morning. I'm going to try her phone one last time and then I'm going to have to report her missing."

"Oh! Do you want me and Dad to help you search for her?"

"I'll let you know." Aron replied. "Speak to you soon."

Chapter Thirty Nine

Esme sat contentedly in the faux leather Travelodge armchair and let Shannon suckle away at her breast. Early that morning the baby's cries had stimulated her breasts to re-lactate straight away, and she wanted the day to go on forever... to hell with the consequences. Her daughter seemed so much more settled on the breast milk she should have had at the start. Esme held Shannon securely in the crook of her arm and stared at the little face, and her own features reflected back. After her feed the baby gave a gentle burp and yawned. For all both of them cared the world outside could have crumbled to dust.

Shannon drifted off to sleep, and Esme laid her carefully down in the pram and covered her with a quilt. She gathered her purse and bag, manoeuvred the pram out of the heavy door to her room, and gave a smile to the middle aged woman monitoring the reception desk. She stepped out of the main door and felt any last vestiges of depression fly swiftly away.

Felixstowe seafront on a cool October afternoon was almost devoid of people, and Esme enjoyed the salty breeze and the chance to be alone with her daughter. She sat under an awning and ate fish and chips out of greaseproof paper, whilst keeping a watchful eye on the pram and its precious occupant. An elderly couple passed by arm-in-arm and the woman glanced at the pram.

"She's got lovely red hair."

"Thank you." Esme smiled in appreciation. "She gets that from her father."

Her father… Billy. Esme decided there and then that she did not really want to think about Billy and Eden; it was enough to just live in the moment and have no other distractions. She finished her meal and threw the fish and chip paper into a nearby bin before resuming her meander along the seafront.

Today her daughter was hers and hers alone. James and Jared would be cared for by their father, and it was only right and proper that she had at least one full day with the baby who would forevermore know her only as Aunt Esme.

Shannon's angelic face begged a photo opportunity. Esme positioned the pram with the beach and sea in the background, then switched on her phone and snapped away.

An incessant and almost immediate buzzing brought her back to reality with a stab of regret. She looked at the display screen and sighed.

"Hello Aron."

"What the fuck's going on? Where are you?"

She held her anger in check.

"I'm having a day out with my daughter. We will be staying overnight at a Travelodge, and then I shall take her back to Ede round about lunchtime tomorrow so that they can have a lie-in. I hope you can give me this time alone with my baby without calling in the police, the Army, and the men carrying white jackets that do up at the back."

"Why didn't you leave a note? The boys are worried, let alone me and your mother. Even my mum and dad are worried as well!"

She could hear the anger in his voice.

"Because you would have immediately come out to find me. My mother would have accompanied you, and so then would the boys. I can assure you I'm perfectly fine, and just want a day and a night with my baby."

"She's not your baby, she's Ede's and Billy's!"

Esme rocked the pram back and forth with one hand, and held on to the phone with the other.

"Aron, nothing can take away the fact that I gave birth to her and therefore I *am* her mother. Just give me this day. It's all I ask."

"And all I ask is that you bring her back to Eden tomorrow morning."

His tone was less angry now. Esme followed a passing cargo ship with her eyes before replying.

"Of course I will! I hope you won't ring her, spill the beans and spoil their day. They're enjoying the wedding, and I'm having a lovely day with Shannon."

"She's called *Julia*."

"Julia then." Esme replied with some irritation. "*Julia, Julia, Julia.*"

A seagull shrieked, and Aron quickly intervened.

"Are you down at Felixstowe?"

"It's none of your damn business *where* I am. Call off the troops and I'll be home in the morning."

She ended the call, took another photo of the baby, then switched off the phone and carried on walking.

***

Esme, wide awake, lay back on the pillows as Shannon suckled, and mused on how time seemed suspended in the small hours of the morning when it felt as though the whole world was fast asleep. As the goodness from her body poured into her daughter, she knew her own milk was the one thing her baby could not do without. Therefore it made sense to her that

Shannon should not struggle any more on soy milk or cow's milk formula that she could obviously not tolerate. Eden was not really coping, and so there was only one thing for it; she would need to persuade Aron to be a father to Billy's baby.

Sated, her daughter yawned and settled down to sleep in her arms. Esme kissed the top of Shannon's forehead and gently laid her down in the pram and covered her over. She noted just two nappies left in the changing bag, and vowed to get an early start back home after breakfast.

Chapter Forty

He parked the car where he could see the entrance to the Travelodge and to where her car stood empty near the main door, and then sat back and waited. At 07:20 the sun had only just appeared over the horizon and picked out a lone dog walker making the most of the early morning along the quiet Felixstowe seafront. Aron poured a cup of coffee from his flask and sipped the warm liquid slowly. Squawking seagulls circled overhead; the same cries he had heard when he had last spoken to her.

As he finished a second cup of coffee there was a flash from her central locking lights. He stepped quickly out of the car and crossed the road as the main door to the Travelodge slid back. He watched Esme as she pushed a pram towards the back of the car, then opened the door and lifted the baby from the pram. He ignored her look of disgust as she spotted him hurrying in her direction.

"What the hell are you doing here? Who's sitting with the boys?"

"Your mother stayed overnight." Aron opened the car boot and began to fold down the pram. "I wanted to make sure you're okay."

He ignored a stab of irritation as she rolled her eyes heavenwards before placing Julia in the car seat.

"Do I look out of my mind? I can assure you I'm perfectly sane. All this baby needed was my breast milk. She hasn't murmured all night. There's been no screaming and no vomiting. Look at her!" Esme pointed with one finger. "She's awake and sitting in the car perfectly quiet! Aron, she needs her mother's milk! She needs to live with *us*!"

On hearing his wife's words he deliberately ignored the baby and shook his head violently.

"No way! I don't want another mouth to feed, and Ez, you're sick in the head if you think Ede and Billy are ever going to allow it! What right have you to take their baby away?"

"*I'm* her mother, not Eden." Esme closed the car door. "Are you going to dispute that? No court would even question that fact!"

"Yeah, but *I'm* not her father." Aron kept his voice even. "Why should I work my arse off keeping Billy's kid?"

"Because she is not being looked after properly, that's why. They're giving her milk that she cannot digest. She's not putting on the right amount of weight. With my milk, she will thrive."

Aron was determined his wife would not have the last word.

"Then you'll have to pump it out and give it to them. In a couple of months she'll be on solids, so all this won't matter."

The steely glint in her eyes told him of her mindset.

"I'm not bloody well driving back and forth to Ipswich all day!"

"And I'm not fucking well keeping someone else's kid!"

His vow to keep his temper had failed. Aron threw the pram in the boot of the car and slammed down the lid as hard as he could.

"I wish you'd never gone through with this! Look what it's done to us!"

He followed her with his eyes as she skirted round him to the driver's door and opened it.

"Well, you'll just have to get on with it. She's my kid, and you're my husband, so that means she's yours as well. Shannon

164

is here to stay now, and she's going to remain with *me*. If you continue to object, that will obviously mean that I have to live elsewhere with her and the twins, so that's what I'll do."

He kicked the offside tyre.

"You'll not take my boys away from me! No way! Get that into your thick skull for a start!"

He inwardly gloated at the sudden look of alarm on her face. A young man and woman wheeling cases behind them exited from the Travelodge. The man stopped in his tracks and stared past him to Esme.

"You alright, love?"

Aron, incensed, strode towards the man.

"Mind your own fucking business!"

Behind him he could hear that Esme had slammed the car door, started the engine, and was backing out of her parking space. The young woman pulled her partner away, and Aron turned around just in time to punch the side window of Esme's car as she drove out into the road.

    ***

He had calmed down somewhat by the time he reached the Newmarket clock tower. Aron turned right at the tower and travelled along Exning Road towards their home in Churchill Avenue, and noticed Janet's car next to Esme's on the driveway. He parked in the road outside, took a deep breath, and turned off the engine. Two little boys threw their arms around him as he opened the front door.

"We went in your bedroom to wake you up, but you and Mummy weren't there!"

Jared's indignation had rubbed off on his brother. James nodded.

"Yeah, Daddy! Nanny was asleep on the settee!"

165

He picked a boy up under each arm and gave each one a squeeze.

"Well, I'm home now, so what are you complaining about?"

"Mummy's here with Julia!" Jared announced excitedly. "She says Julia's going to live with us and that we've got a sister now!"

She had already got the boys on her side. Aron sighed and shook his head.

"Julia is your cousin. She's Aunty Ede and Uncle Billy's baby. I'm going to phone them straight away and tell them to come over and get her."

Their features appeared crestfallen, and they struggled to free themselves from his grip. Aron put his sons down.

"Go up to your room and play for a bit. I'll take you swimming at the leisure centre a bit later on."

Happier, the boys ran upstairs. Aron took out his mobile phone from his pocket, tapped in a message to both Eden and Billy, then went into the front room. A united front of Esme and Janet regarded him with distaste. He back-tracked to the kitchen and put some bread in the toaster, arriving at the conclusion that some plain speaking needed to be done, and very soon.

Chapter Forty One

A buzz brought her back to consciousness. Eden reached over to the bedside table and picked up her phone, noticing that the time read 09:15; she had not slept so long in ages.

"Billy…Billy…wake up!"

"W..What?" Billy rubbed his eyes. "What's wrong?"

Eden shoved Aron's message in front of Billy's face.

"Look! Aron says we've got to go over and pick up Julia as soon as we can!"

Irritated at his inability to function, Eden leaped out of bed.

"There might be something wrong with her!"

Billy sat up sleepily.

"More likely she's screamed all night and they're at the end of their tether."

She put on a dressing gown and made for the door.

"I'm going to have a shower. There's some bacon in the fridge if you want a sandwich. Can you make me a coffee please?"

She had the quickest wash she had ever had, then threw on some jeans, a jumper and trainers and ran downstairs, irritated to find Billy still in his dressing gown.

"Thanks for the drink. Can you hurry up a bit?" She took a gulp of coffee. "They're waiting for us."

***

The front door opened as she walked towards it, and Aron came out to stand on the porch.

"Hi."

Billy overtook her.

"What the hell's up? We were still in bed!"

"The baby's fine, but we all need to have a talk. Something needs to be brought out in the open."

Esme appeared behind Aron, and Eden began to worry. She stepped into the hallway, noticing how her mother had hold of both twins' hands.

"I'm taking the boys upstairs for now. They're going to help me bath Julia."

"Has she been sick again?" Eden listened for her daughter's cry, but could hear nothing. "Can I see her?"

"She's fine. I'll just get her dressed." Janet gave a quick glance at Aron. "She's in her seat upstairs, but the kids and I are going to leave you four to it. Come up when you've had your little talk."

Eden followed the others into the front room, and took a seat on the settee next to Billy. Esme, still silent, sank into an armchair opposite, and Aron sat down cross-legged on the floor.

Billy was the first to speak.

"What's all this about?"

Eden noticed a quick glance between her sister and Aron. A hundred catastrophes flashed through her mind in an instant.

"Are you sure Julia's okay?"

"She's never been better." Esme replied quietly. "She's had no colic, sickness, or diarrhoea. She's slept all night ... and do you know why?"

Eden smiled

"Oh, that's great! Why?"

"Because I've been breast-feeding her. She's been drinking her natural mother's milk."

In a flash Eden's heart sank with the sure and certain knowledge of what would come next. She sighed.

"You were supposed to give her the bottles of soya milk formula in the fridge."

"How's Ede going to compete with that?" Billy stared at Esme and stood up angrily. "You're not giving her a bloody chance!"

"Sit down, mate." Aron gestured with one hand in a downwards motion. "I'm on your side, believe me."

Pacified for the moment, Billy exhaled forcefully and resumed a seated position. Eden grabbed hold of Billy's hand as Esme continued, eyes downcast.

"I'm keeping Shannon. I can't give her up."

Eden drew in a deep breath and tears filled her eyes. Billy shook his head.

"Over my dead body! I'll drag you through the courts! You can't have it all your own fucking way! She's *my* kid as well!"

"You can't do this to me, Ez!" Eden sobbed. "You've already got the twins! You promised you'd give her to *me*!"

Esme put her head in her hands.

"I thought I could do it, but I can't." She shook her head. "I can't give away my baby… I just can't do it. Could *you*?"

Eden, panicked now, jumped up from the settee and ran out into the hallway, taking the stairs two at a time.

"Mum! Mum! Give me Julia!"

She rattled the handle of the bathroom door, which refused to budge. From behind the door came the sounds of the boys' murmurs and happy splashes. Janet's voice sounded from the other side of the door.

"Aron's told me to wait until you've all discussed it. Sorry darling, but I have to be neutral on this."

Deflated, Eden crumpled into a heap on the top step and eyes closed, rocked to and fro.

"No! Please don't take away my baby!" She sobbed. "I want her *so* much! I've waited so long to be a mother!"

She heard Billy's footsteps on the stairs, and felt his arms around her.

"Come on, let's go back down. Aron doesn't want to keep Julia, I can tell. Perhaps he'll get Ez to change her mind."

"She won't." Eden wiped her eyes. "I know my sister."

"Then we'll go through the courts and we'll fight for custody. Come down for now. We've got to talk this through."

Reluctantly she followed Billy. She sat down heavily on the settee, while a hush settled momentarily over the room. Aron stood up and began to pace up and down.

"I don't want to spend my life working to keep another man's kid, I've already told Ez that, but I've got to live with her and there's no way she's ever going to be happy again at this rate unless she keeps the baby."

"But it's okay for Ede to be depressed then?" Billy stared at Aron. "She's even given up her job! We'd never have gone through with this if we thought Ez was going to change her mind!"

"I'm so sorry." Esme sighed. "I feel a total and utter shit for doing this, but I can't go on pretending that everything's fine, because it's *not*."

Billy stood up.

"Get yourself a good lawyer, 'cos you're going to need one. See you in court. Come on Ede, let's go."

Eden stood up, wiped her eyes, and dazedly followed Billy out to the car.

Chapter Forty Two

Aron could already see Billy through the office window as he guided his motorbike in through the yard gates and turned off the engine. As he took off his crash helmet he was surprised to see Billy striding towards him.

"Just want to say this…"

"What?" Aron sighed at the thought of another confrontation. He put his bike on its stand and took off his leather jacket.

"We've got to work together. We've got a good business going here, so we at least need to be on speaking terms. We can't let what happened the other day spoil what we've got *here*."

"Listen, mate." Aron chucked his jacket on the seat of his bike. "I agree with what you're saying, but I want to add that it's no use trying to gain custody of the baby via the courts. I've spoken to a solicitor friend of Barry's, who says it's unlikely you'll win unless you can prove that Esme is an unfit mother. You might have to pay legal fees as well. Shannon's thriving on Esme's milk and they bonded straight away… you know that, don't you?"

Billy nodded.

"I was angry. We're *both* angry at Ez for going back on her word. To be honest, I don't think Eden will ever talk to Esme again. Ez will have to be prepared for that."

Aron put an arm around Billy's shoulder as they walked towards the office.

"She knows, and she'll have to live with it. Do check out what I've said though. I'm trying to avoid you having another big disappointment along with solicitor's bills as well."

"I'm the kid's father." Billy opened the door to the office. "I *will* check it all out because it would be nice if Ede and I could be awarded visiting rights."

Aron closed the office door behind them.

"Christ, mate. If we can get the girls to start talking to each other again you can visit any time you bloody well like! It makes sense, yeah? But no judge in this country is going to take a baby that's thriving from its birth mother. Ez and I are her legal parents and all of us will have to get used to that. Under the circumstances I don't expect you to pay for her upkeep... I can't be fairer than that, but just leave the courts out of it, eh? Shit...if Ede doesn't want to know, then come on your own and visit us whenever you want. How does that all sound?"

He was relieved when after a few moments' hesitation, Billy nodded.

"I *will* check out what you've said, but hey, it all sounds fair. Cheers."

***

It was a pleasure to come home to a happy house. He took off his crash helmet, revved the engine of his bike on the driveway with his right hand and waved to Esme, holding Shannon, with his left. He smiled as his two little sons rushed out of the front door.

"Daddy! Can we sit on your bike?"

He laughed, turned off the engine and pulled the bike back on its stand.

"Come on then."

"I'm sitting in the front!" James shouted.

"I don't care." Jared climbed into the pillion seat. "Daddy will let me have a go in a minute."

"Daddy wants his dinner." Aron replied with a laugh. "So hurry up James and have your go."

Esme came towards him with the baby asleep in her arms.

"How'd it go with Billy today?"

He lifted Jared over James' head.

"Move back, James." He put Jared in the front seat and turned to Esme.

"I advised him it's hopeless trying to gain custody, but told him he can come and see Shannon any time he likes. Billy's her father so it's only fair that we let him visit. It doesn't look as though Ede will though. You've burned your bridges there." He saw her face fall at the mention of her sister. "You can't blame her, Ez."

"I know." Esme nodded. "I've let her down badly."

He lifted one boy under each arm, and walked towards the house.

"Billy's taken me up on my offer, so he'll start turning up sooner or later I'm sure. What's for dinner?"

"Vegetable pizza!" James yelled in his ear.

"And pasta!" Jared shrieked.

"That's it... tell the whole street!" Aron chuckled. "You two need your volume controls turning down."

He deposited the boys at the doorstep, and gave Esme a kiss on the cheek.

"One thing's bothering me..."

"What's that?" She looked at him with interest.

"What shall we tell Shannon about her father?"

"I haven't thought about that yet." Esme shrugged. "I guess we'll cross that bridge when we come to it."

"I think we ought to tell her straight away when she can talk and understand, so that she grows up with the knowledge."

Esme shook her head.

"No, it's best to wait until she's older, about ten or eleven. I'll tell Billy not to say anything. It'll be upsetting for a little tot to wonder why her daddy lives somewhere else. At least when she's older we can reason with her and explain all the circumstances surrounding her birth."

"Hmm... have it your way." Aron made his way to the kitchen. "But I think you're making a big mistake."

Chapter Forty Three

Most of her immediate family was lost to her now; her sister, little Julia, her brother-in-law, and her two nephews. She could never visit their house again. Eden was grateful of her mother's constant presence and support, as she battled dark days of depression and emptiness.

"You need something to fill your time, Ede." Janet skipped through the local newspaper. "Have a look in the job vacancies to see if there's something you fancy."

Eden looked out the back window at bare trees and a frost-covered lawn. She felt as cold and dead inside as a December garden; in a kind of permanent hibernation in order to avoid the reality of life without Julia. She had come to realise that sleep afforded the best escape; sleep, and ever-increasing glasses of wine when nobody could see.

"Who'd want *me*?" She wailed, on the verge of tears. "I'm no good to anybody."

Janet thrust the newspaper in Eden's direction.

"Young lady, if I hear you say that one more time I'm out of here! The council is advertising, as somebody is going on maternity leave at your library. Why don't you apply to cover their job?"

"I can't face them all again." Eden sniffed. "I feel such a failure."

"If you don't apply, I'm going to ask the GP to come round here and prescribe you some happy pills. Do you want that?"

"No." Eden sighed. "I don't."

"Then apply for the job. If not *that* job, then *any* job. Do it for *me*." Janet gave her a nudge. "You'll thank me one day."

***

Eden could feel her ex-colleagues' eyes boring through the librarian's office window.

"So I'm here to ask if you are willing to take me back on please? My sister in her wisdom decided to keep the baby, and that was the last chance for me to be a mother. There won't be another. I'm going out of my mind sitting at home all day, and so I'd like to come back on a permanent basis and in the meantime apply to cover Ferne's maternity leave."

Lionel Wood regarded the serious-looking woman in front of him.

"As you know it will be the council's decision and you will have to apply all over again, but I'll be happy to give you a good reference as you were an excellent worker. I have an application form here for you to take away."

"Thank you." Eden managed a thin smile as she reached over to take the form. "I really appreciate it."

On her way out she acknowledged Ferne and Susan at the desk. There was another face she did not recognise, a young woman perhaps in her late twenties who presumably had been employed to take over when she had left, full of expectation and excitement. Eden sighed, avoided the sight of Ferne's burgeoning belly, and made haste for the exit.

***

She hated Friday evenings, and after being accepted back at the library she would always elect to work the late shift. Billy would disappear, and she knew where he was off to. He would return in a happier mood, and with yet more photos on his phone. She knew that for a fact because she would always sneak a peek

176

at Julia when he was in the shower. There she was … red-headed Julia smiling, attempting to crawl, eating, sleeping, and being held in a loving embrace by her natural father. Despite an insatiable curiosity, she never asked him about the baby, and no information was ever forthcoming. In her parents' house she feasted her eyes on photos of Julia on the walls and mused on how much the baby's hair resembled Billy's; she was pleased about that, as otherwise the resemblance to her sister was uncanny.

She often wondered whether her sense of loss would ever ease. As a distraction therapy and to avoid a visit to the GP with the resulting possible addiction to Sertraline, she threw herself into her work and studied hard for her librarian's exams. The hatred she felt towards her sister stayed constant, and she soon became used to not having Esme in her life.

Chapter Forty Four

Esme regarded Marcia McKinnon across the coffee table.

"I'm back again. I didn't think I'd need the third appointment, but now I do for a different reason."

"It's nice to see you again." Marcia smiled at Esme. "What's been going on in your life? Would you like to bring me up to date?"

Esme sighed.

"Oh, I don't know where to start! I have the baby, but of course my sister now refuses to speak to me or have anything to do with me at all. Instead of making her happy, which was my initial intention, I've made her hate me with a vengeance. I can't give the baby up. I don't know why I've come here. I know you can't help me, but hey... I came anyway."

It was good to get it all off her chest. She exhaled with relief and watched Marcia sit back in her chair and cross her legs.

"It's always good to talk to somebody outside the family and get a different perspective on things. How has your sister's attitude made you feel?"

"Awful." Esme wiped away a tear. "Sometimes I can't sleep at night as I feel so guilty. Eden's husband visits on Fridays to see Shannon, but he never mentions my sister."

"Have you tried testing the water with him regarding Eden? Perhaps ask him how she's doing?"

Esme shook her head.

"There's a wall in place that I'll never get over. Billy is perfectly friendly and approachable, but I know he doesn't want me to see Eden and make his wife upset all over again. I did try asking once, but he blanked me and changed the subject."

Marcia nodded.

"Perhaps in time there may be a thaw in relations? You see your brother-in-law on a regular basis, and so when enough water has gone under the bridge your sister may come around and want to be part of Shannon's life. You never know."

"Eden's stubborn." Esme looked over at Marcia. "I *know* her. She'll never be the first one to make amends."

"Then you must try harder to achieve your goal. If I had a sister, then that's what I would do. Don't give up on Eden, just keep at it. Send her a letter maybe. Write and tell her how you feel."

Sometimes she felt as though she could cry for England. Esme wiped her eyes and took a sip of water.

"Did you ever watch *The Godfather*?"

"Of course." Marcia nodded. "Most people have seen that one."

"Remember when Fredo went against the family and was shunned by Michael? It's like that I think. My sister is a very determined person."

"Perhaps her husband will take photos of the baby and she will change her mind." Marcia replied. "Don't give up hope."

Esme smiled.

"It's nice to talk to somebody about it. I *know* Aron thinks it's all my own fault, but I just can't give that baby up. I carried for nine months and gave birth to her. I'm her *mother*."

Marcia nodded.

"At the end of the day we must live true to ourselves, no matter what the cost."

Part Two, Chapter Forty Five
2013

James had pulled Susie's arm off again. Five year old Shannon tearfully held up her prized dolly in Jared's direction.

"Mend it."

"*Please*." Jared kicked his brother and took the doll. "Did you do this, James?"

"Please." Shannon wailed in a pleading tone. "*Please. Please. Please.*"

James returned Jared's kick with one of his own and then punched the doll out of his brother's hand.

. "Okay, don't overdo it. Nothing to do with me."

"Mummy! James hurted Susie!"

Her mother could always make things better. Shannon stuck out her tongue at James.

"I hate you!"

"I hate you too, ginger nut." James whispered in her ear. "Why don't you go back and live with Uncle Billy? Everything was fine until *you* came along. You're *not* my sister."

Shannon, confused, gave James a stare as their mother came into the room.

"What's going on?"

"James hurted Susie."

"James *hurt* Susie." Esme corrected.

"How do *you* know?" James retorted indignantly. "You weren't there."

"Process of elimination, brother." Jared wrenched the TV remote from his brother's hand. "It definitely wasn't Shannon, and I *know* it wasn't me. Dad's at work, Mum's been talking on the phone, and so that leaves *you*, Dipstick."

Jared snatched back the remote control.

"It's my turn to pick."

"The two of you pack it in!" Esme's voice rose. "Shannon, why don't you come outside with me and play in the garden?"

"Yeah, why doesn't she? "James flicked through several channels. "She follows us around, like, *all the time*."

Jared repaired the doll's injured limb.

"There you go, Shannon. Susie's mended now."

Shannon grinned at the brother she loved with all her heart.

"Thank you."

She wanted to watch *Blue Peter*, but James obviously had other ideas. Her wheedling might have worked with Jared, but with James she did not have a chance. Shannon held Susie close to her chest, and followed her mother out of the room.

"Can you take the lid off the sandpit, Mummy?"

Shannon took off her socks and shoes and ran out onto the lawn, where she saw her mother heading towards the sandpit. She put Susie down on a sun lounger then picked up a bucket and spade that she had left on the patio the previous evening. She ran over to her mother and jumped into the open sandpit.

"James said he wanted me to go back and live with Uncle Billy. Did I used to live with Uncle Billy?"

She noticed her mother's fleeting expression of surprise.

"No, of course you didn't. Don't take any notice of what he says."

Mollified, Shannon slowly filled up a small bucket with sand.

"Can I watch *Blue Peter*?"

She was dismayed when her mother shook her head.

"Not just yet. I'm recording it for you though. It's James' turn for now."

"I don't like James." Shannon turned the bucket of sand over. "He says I'm not his sister."

She heard a small intake of breath from her mother.

"I will speak to him. He's naughty to tell lies like that."

Shannon nodded in agreement and tapped the top of the bucket with the spade.

"Why doesn't he like me?"

She lifted the bucket upwards to expose a perfectly formed sandcastle.

"Look what I've made, Mummy!"

"Well done." Esme smiled. "James gets a bit annoyed sometimes. It's just the way he is, but he still loves you I know."

Shannon smashed the spade into the sandcastle and demolished it. She knew James hated her despite what her mother had said, but that was okay because she hated him as well.

Chapter Forty Six

Esme muted the sound and gave Jared the remote control.

"It's your turn now. Another half hour of TV, then dinner and homework. James, can you come out to the kitchen please. I want a word with you."

She closed the kitchen door behind them, checked out the window at Shannon playing in the sandpit, then looked at the sulky face of her teenage son and sighed.

"I thought I told you not to say anything to Shannon about the circumstances surrounding her birth."

James had lost the blond cuteness of his boyhood. Acne had erupted in a trail across his forehead and cheeks, and his hair had darkened to a few shades above her own mousey brown. Esme positioned herself against the door to guard against James' possible quick escape.

"She gets on my nerves. Wherever we go, then *there she is*. We don't want a five year old following us around all the time!"

"Well, Jared doesn't have a problem with it." Esme replied with a shrug. "She *is* your sister, and I don't want you telling her otherwise. If you can't treat her nicely, then your pocket money will be taken away and you can stay here with Shannon on Saturdays instead of helping out at the yard."

She was relieved to see her words had hit home.

"O...kay..."

"Good." Esme nodded. "I've made myself clear then?"

"Crystal." James' grey eyes bored into hers. "I remember though that you were supposed to have her for Aunty Eden who I haven't seen for years. Why did Shannon come back here?"

A searing dismay shot through Esme at her son's powers of recollection.

"It's not anything you need to concern yourself with. Shannon is my daughter and your sister, and that's all you need to know."

"Fine." James replied brusquely. "Can I go now?"

She moved aside, wanting so much to hug the son who was moving inexorably away from her control.

***

Life was not turning out quite as she had hoped. Esme took the cup from her mother's hand and gave a wry smile.

"Thanks for this. I wish a cup of tea could solve everything."

"It's supposed to." Janet Prentice chuckled. "What's the problem?"

"Oh…it's James really. Since Shannon joined the family I think he's had his nose put out of joint. She loves Jared and so follows the pair of them about. It gets a bit tense sometimes. Maybe I made a big mistake? Maybe I should never have taken her from Eden?"

"Too late." Janet shook her head. "Too late to uproot Shannon. You'll do more harm than good if you do that. The child is settled with you now."

"It's hard being a mother, isn't it?" Esme sighed. "All I ever wanted to do was get it right."

Janet took a few sips of tea before continuing.

"We learn as we go along. With hindsight there are things that we all could have done better."

"Amen to that." Esme agreed. "It's just that the family dynamics have been… well… disrupted."

Janet nodded.

"Your main problem is that the boys were old enough to remember what went on at the time. I expect James resents Shannon for upsetting the status quo, so to speak. Maybe you'll have to give him more attention. Praise him up if he does something nice."

"But he doesn't!" Esme rolled her eyes. "Jared's fine, but with James it's always dramas and meltdowns, sulking and stomping."

Janet laughed.

"Sounds like a fourteen year old to me. Take him out, just on his own. I'll sit with Shannon. Do something nice with him. The more you shout at him about Shannon, the more he'll resent you and her."

"Oh, God, give me strength." Esme drained her cup. "Why can't I have a normal family like everybody else?"

Janet shrugged.

"Who can guarantee that other families are normal?"

***

"Is it cool being out with your mother?"

She took her eyes off the road briefly to be rewarded with a hint of a smile.

"No." James replied. "I hope my mates don't see me. Where are we going?"

"Somewhere where they're not. We're going to the Riverside Leisure Centre at Chelmsford."

"Why? What's there?"

She waggled one finger.

"Ah, that's for me to know and you to wonder about."

For once the silence between them was not toxic. When the Riverside Centre came into view, Esme parked the car.

"Come on then. We're going ice skating. I haven't been here for years. I bet I can get round the rink faster than you."

There was no reply from James. She could see him taking in his surroundings as they queued to pay for skate hire. Finally as they stood together at the counter he exhaled forcefully and whispered under his breath.

"I can't do this."

"How do you know?" Esme replied as she handed over their shoes and took two pairs of skates from the assistant. "We've never taken you here before. Give it a try for ten minutes. If you don't like it, then we'll go home. I can't say fairer than that."

She marched ahead to a bench and sat down, aware that he had hung behind. She bent forward and slipped her foot into one boot.

"Come on, James. It's fun. Come and put your skates on."

With some reluctance he complied, much to her relief.

"Now the fun bit starts when you stand up and try and walk on them."

To her surprise he got to his feet straight away.

"Bring it on. Easy peasy."

Together they clomped through the alleyway to the rink. Expert skaters performed jumps and spins before her eyes, whilst beginners held on grimly to the side rails. Esme grinned at James.

"Easy, you say? Show me how easy it is then!"

She glided onto the ice, hoping against hope her 37 year old body would not fail her. She took a long step and promptly fell flat onto her backside. Her son's laughter was music to her ears.

"Oh, I haven't fallen over for years! She got clumsily to her feet. "I'll have you know I was the skater queen of Streatham when I was your age."

"*Where*?" James held on to the rail. "Where's Streatham?"

Esme brushed the ice off her clothes.

"In South East London, where I grew up. Come on, show me what you can do."

She skated gingerly away from the side and held out her hand. To her surprise James' took a step and his hand clasped around her own.

"Let's see if we can get once around without breaking our legs."

She ignored the skaters whooshing past her ears, and concentrated on enjoying the moment. When they had completed a full circuit, she could tell that James had liked the experience.

"This is cool!"

Her confidence on the ice returned at the same time that James picked up speed.

"Can you bring Jared and me here again? I can give him a race!"

Esme chuckled.

"Yeah, but first you've got to race *me*!"

Twenty years flew away in a flash. Esme took off with vigour, but when she checked behind she realised her mistake. Her crash into the side wall was an unwelcome surprise.

"That was spectacular!" James skated up to her and held out his hand. "Come on Mum, let's have another go."

Bruised but undaunted, Esme got shakily to her feet.

"I'm not going to be able to walk tomorrow."

"You'll never beat me anyway." James laughed. "So give it up. Watch the expert."

She stood against the rail and with a smile followed him around the rink with her eyes. Her mother had been right; all James had needed was a bit more attention. Jared was easy-going, but James was a bit more highly strung and she had made the mistake of lumping them both together. She resolved there and then to try to do all she could to build a better relationship with all three of her children. She would need to speak to Aron too about his tendency to favour the boys over Shannon. It was time to head away from becoming the dysfunctional family unit that she saw so often in newspapers and on TV.

James skidded to a halt beside her.

"Can I have a pair of ice skates, please?"

Esme chuckled.

"I thought you said you couldn't skate? Well, maybe it's time to get that paper round you've always wriggled out of doing. Perhaps when you buy your own skates, you'll take good care of them. Think of all the tips you'll get at Christmas."

"Yeah, but it means I'll have to get up early." James pulled a face. "Micky at school has to get up at six o'clock."

"So what?" Esme shrugged and moved away from the rail. "It won't kill you. I've been getting up at six o'clock for years."

"Yeah, but you're ...old."

Esme picked up speed on the ice.

"Yeah, I'm ancient... but I can skate faster than *you*!"

It was exhilarating flashing past learners like she used to do. Esme hoped against hope that she did not fall flat on her arse again.

Chapter Forty Seven

Aron hated those four words *we have to talk.* It usually meant he was in for a bollicking. He took off his crash helmet and waved at the boys as they tinkered with their bicycles in the garage.

"Hi Dad!" Jared stood up. "I've got a puncture."

Aron glanced at the upended bike.

"I taught you how to mend it. If you have any trouble, come and get me. I'll just say hello to Mum and have a cup of tea first."

His son gave a thumbs up sign.

"Okay."

Aron walked into the hallway. The usual sound of children's TV was absent.

"Hi!" He shouted. "I'm home!"

He smiled at Esme as she came out to meet him.

"Hi. You got my text?"

"Yeah." He nodded. "What have I done this time?"

"Come and sit in the garden. Shannon is at a friend's house for tea. I just wanted to mention something while we've got a minute to ourselves."

Aron removed his Kevlar jacket and over-trousers and went out the back door into the garden. He sat down on a bench and hoped it wouldn't be too long before one of his sons wanted him for bicycle repair. Presently Esme walked towards him carrying a laden tray.

"The chicken and roast potatoes are cooking. All I've got to do is put the veggies in the steamer."

"Come on then, Fanny Craddock." Aron took a steaming cup of tea from the tray. "Out with it."

Esme laughed.

"Who's Fanny Craddock?"

He moved along the bench and Esme sat down next to him.

"It's Shannon. I can't help but notice that you tend to favour the boys over her."

He took a gulp of tea.

"I should think that's bloody obvious why, isn't it?" He replied testily. "She's not my kid. I took her on because I love *you*. I did it for *you*."

"I know that." Esme nodded. "And I'm grateful, don't get me wrong, but now she's getting older she's going to notice how you treat her."

Aron swallowed a rising irritation.

"Remember Arletta in *Cool Hand Luke*? She got it right when she said sometimes you have a feeling for a child and sometimes you don't. How can I have the same feelings for her that I do for my own sons? She's Billy's daughter, not mine. Have you seen those farm programmes? Sheep for instance reject any lamb that's not theirs."

"Yes, but our brains are more developed than those of sheep." Esme replied quietly. "Sooner or later she'll pick up on your negative vibes. She's a girl, and girls are more sensitive like that."

Aron sighed; the weight of the world on his shoulders.

"I'll do my best, but whenever I look at her I see Billy. Any bloke looking at her will know she's not mine."

I know." Esme nodded. "But just try, eh?"

190

Aron shrugged.

"I'll try, that's all I can say. I'm more at home with soldiers, guns, robots and cars then I am with dollies and make up. She talks too much, and it's all *shite*."

Esme gave a *tut* of annoyance.

"She's five years old for God's sake! They boys talked shite at five!"

"Yeah, they did." Aron agreed. "But she never *stops* talking."

Esme turned towards him.

"Little girls chatter. I did. Eden did, and now Shannon does. Try and spend some time with her. Take her to the park on Sunday mornings while I cook the dinner. Teach her how to swim... all the things you used to do with the boys."

"Billy should be doing this, not me." Aron grumbled. "It would be nice to have sex with my wife on a Sunday morning."

"Billy comes round to see her every Friday without fail. As for the sex, *who* had to wake *whom* up at eleven o'clock last Sunday?"

"Only because I'd been out with the lads."

"Yeah, well...perhaps it's time to go out with your little girl instead."

Aron leaned back on the bench and closed his eyes. He had swiftly come to the conclusion that his preference would more likely be for repairing a bicycle tyre than for dressing up a dolly. He had no idea on how to go about being a father to someone else's daughter.

"What do I do with her?"

Esme sighed.

"Love her, for God's sake. Just love her."

Part Three, Chapter Forty Eight
2019

Through the net curtains she watched as Shannon waved goodbye to her friends and then jumped off the school bus, a flame of red hair flying upwards. She smiled as her daughter ran up the garden path and burst in through the front door.

"Hey Mum, I'm home!"

"Hello, love." Esme came out into the hallway. "Had a good day at school?"

Shannon grimaced.

"No, it was boring, and now I've got to do homework!"

"Ah well, settle down and get it over with." Esme shrugged. "What subject?"

Shannon threw down her school bag and flung off her coat, leaving both on the floor.

"Science. It's about inheriting genes and stuff from your family. Can I have a biscuit?"

Esme followed Shannon into the kitchen with a sudden twinge of unease.

"Can I have a biscuit, *please.*"

"Oh yeah…" Shannon jumped up onto a stool. "*Please.*"

Esme took out two biscuits from the tin and poured out a glass of milk.

"Here you are… that'll do until dinner time."

Shannon picked up the first biscuit and looked at Esme thoughtfully.

"We did hair colour and eye colour today. So how come I've got ginger hair like Uncle Billy and the boys have blond hair like Dad's? Miss Tucker says we inherit stuff from both parents. What have I got from Dad then?"

Esme, suddenly nervous, sat down opposite Shannon.

"I've been wanting to tell you for a while now, but was not sure how to go about it."

Shannon took a bite of her biscuit.

"Tell me what?"

"It's about Uncle Billy. Uncle Billy is married to Aunty Eden, the aunt you've never met."

"Yeah?" Shannon shrugged. "So what?"

"Well…a few years back she had to have an operation which made her unable to have children. She really wanted children, and was terribly sad that she couldn't have any."

She had the child's full attention, she could tell. Esme sighed and carried on.

"So … I offered to have a baby for her."

"Where is it then?" Shannon paused in mid-chew. "Where's the baby?"

Esme rested her fingers over Shannon's free hand.

"*You. You* were the baby. Uncle Billy is your birth father, not Dad, but I loved you so much that I couldn't give you up. Do you remember when I told you how babies are made?"

"You don't have to go through *that* again!" Shannon rolled her eyes. "I'm not stupid!"

"Well, it was Uncle Billy's seed that made you and not Daddy's. That's why you've got red hair like him."

Shannon inched away from her mother.

"I've never even *seen* Aunty Eden!"

"No". Replied Esme. "And neither have I since you were a baby. She was angry that I kept you. I think she's probably still angry. She's never wanted to come here because of what I did to her."

"I don't blame her!" Shannon stood up, spitting bits of biscuit over the table. "You took her baby away! Aunty Eden was supposed to be my mother! I was supposed to live with *them*!"

To Esme's horror, Shannon burst into tears and ran up the stairs. She had known the time would soon come for Shannon to be told about the circumstances surrounding her birth, but had been unprepared for that particular moment. Esme jumped up from her chair and took the stairs two at a time. Over the years she had put Shannon's parentage to the back of her mind as she had not wanted to rock the boat. However, now the moment of truth had suddenly arrived, and she had to deal with the fallout.

Chapter Forty Nine

Shannon slammed her bedroom door as hard as she could.

"I hate you!"

On the landing she could hear her mother's footsteps come to a stop outside her door. Shannon turned the key in the lock and dragged a chair under the doorknob for good measure.

"Go away!"

Life was so unfair! She was stuck with a mother who told her lies and a father who never seemed interested in anything she did or said. Shannon wanted to scream. The nicest people in the *whole world* were Jared and her uncle Billy. But no, now Jared *wasn't* her brother, and her uncle Billy *wasn't* her uncle... *he was her father*! How the hell could she have two fathers?

She flung herself face down upon her bed and let the tears fall. Her mother's voice rose louder as she pushed her weight against the door.

"Shannon! If you don't open this door I shall phone Dad to come home from work and kick it down!"

"Which Dad?" Shannon yelled. "I've got two now, remember?"

"Both of them!"

Her mother meant business. Shannon reluctantly climbed off the bed, moved the chair away from the door and unlocked it. Her mother stood there red-faced and slightly breathless.

"Thank you! Now will you let me explain instead of running off and having a meltdown?"

"Who are *you*?" Shannon wiped her eyes. "Are you really my mother? I can't believe anything you say now!"

She stomped back into the bedroom and sat on the edge of her bed. Her mother sat down beside her and put an arm around her shoulder. Shannon pushed it away.

"Yes, I am your mother. I gave birth to you. You've seen photos of me when I was pregnant."

"S-so why have I got two fathers?" Shannon's voice came in sobs. "Everybody else has got one!"

"I just told you...your Aunty Eden, Uncle Billy's wife, couldn't have children. I offered to have a baby for them, but I loved you so much that I kept you."

"Well, I want to *live* with Aunty Eden and Uncle Billy!" Shannon stood up. "Anywhere's better than living *here*! You've lied to me all these years! When Uncle Billy comes on Friday I'm going to ask if I can stay with *him*!"

She enjoyed seeing her mother's expression change to one of horror.

"You *can't*. You can visit of course if you really want to, but Aunty Eden's a librarian and works long hours, and so does Uncle Billy. There would be nobody at home to look after you."

"I'm not a baby anymore!" Shannon cried. "I don't need looking after!"

She made a point to keep eye contact, and felt a small thrill tingle up her spine when her mother looked away first.

"They live in Ipswich. How are you going to get to school in Newmarket every morning? The school bus doesn't go out that far."

She ignored the note of triumph in her mother's voice.

"They can take me in the car."

"I don't think so. Like I said… they have to go to work. You would have to start at a different school and make new friends."

Shannon thought of Ellie and Marie, her besties. She shook her head.

"I'm not going to a new school."

"Well, you'll have to stay here then, and for your information I haven't lied to you about anything. I decided to tell you now about your dad because you're eleven and I thought you were old enough to understand."

Shannon looked at her mother in disgust.

"Oh yeah, I understand all right! My uncle is my dad, and the one I *thought* was my dad is …. who?"

She ignored her mother's irritated sigh.

"He's my husband and your dad for all intents and purposes…okay, your step-dad. He's the one who earns the money to buy your food and clothes and to keep a roof over your head. He treats you just the same as he does your brothers."

"No he doesn't!" Shannon retorted at once. "He's never been interested in anything I'm doing at school! I can tell! It's always Jared this, or James that… and that figures because now he's not my real dad! Oh God!" She clapped a hand to her mouth. "They're not my real brothers then, are they?"

A fresh river of tears fell down her cheeks. She hung her head and sobbed.

"How could you do that to me? How could you tell me James and Jared are my brothers when they're not? Now I know why James used to tell me I wasn't his sister! I thought he was just being horrible, but he was telling the truth!"

She moved off the bed towards the window and, tried to pretend her mother was not in the room.

"They're your half-brothers. All three of you have the same mother, *me*. I told them not to say anything until you were old enough to deal with it, but obviously James couldn't help himself at the time. I did have a word with him about it, and he stopped … at least I *think* he did. He was jealous when you arrived. That's why he said the things he did."

"Go away!" She replied with venom. "I hate you. I want to go and see Aunty Eden! I bet she's tons better than *you*! Why have you stopped me from seeing her?"

She turned her back on her mother and stared out of the window. Presently she heard the springs on her bed squeak.

"I haven't stopped her, it was *her* idea never to visit. Anyway, have it your own way…I'll arrange a visit when Uncle Billy comes round on Friday."

Her mother's voice sounded strained. Footsteps went out of the door and down the stairs. Shannon put her head on the coolness of the window sill and wept bitter tears of confusion. Her whole world had just been turned upside down. She had heard kids at school talking about *step* mums and *step* dads, and now it had happened to *her*. She couldn't believe it; nothing in her life seemed real anymore.

Chapter Fifty

Eden put her book down and turned off the bedside light when she heard Billy's key in the lock. For the past eleven and a half years he had never spoken of Julia, and she had long ago come to the conclusion that it was pointless to ask.

She willed sleep to send her into unconsciousness. Instead she listened to the toilet flush, the cascade of water in the shower, and Billy's teeth cleaning routing which put her own teeth on edge. When he slipped into bed beside her, she inched away from his cold body.

"Sorry, I'll warm up in a minute." He wriggled under the duvet. "Come and give us a cuddle."

She shifted over to his side, laid her head on his chest and one arm across his middle. He kissed her forehead.

"I've got some news for you."

She looked up at him.

"News? What news?"

"You're going to have a visitor tomorrow afternoon when I've finished at the yard. I'll be bringing somebody home for tea."

She hardly dared to think whom it might be.

"Who?"

"Shannon, and don't call her Julia, for Pete's sake. I made that mistake once. She won't thank you for it."

Eden felt her heart begin to race.

"Why is she coming here after all this time?"

She felt a flash of excitement combined with dread. She snuggled closer and he gave her a squeeze.

"She wants to meet you. Esme's finally told her who her dad is, and the kid's confused and sounding off. She wants to live with us, but of course that's out of the question."

"She wants to meet *me*?" Eden sat up, open-mouthed.

"Sure." Billy yawned. "Why wouldn't she? She can't wait to meet the wicked auntie that nobody's ever seen or talked about."

She chuckled.

"Wow, so I'm back in favour then?"

"With Shannon, yeah." Billy nodded. "Esme didn't put up any barriers, and Aron's all for it."

"Good God." Eden lay back down and stared up at the ceiling. "I'm never going to sleep tonight now."

"Perhaps you need a little bit of exercise before bed? How about some horizontal jogging?"

She laughed as he rolled on top of her.

***

The chocolate sponge cake had turned out just right. Eden, pleased with her efforts, took off her apron and made her way upstairs to the bathroom for a quick shower and hair wash before Billy returned. Nervousness caused her stomach to roll and pitch, and she felt certain she would not be able to eat a thing at tea time.

Wearing her best dress and after the umpteenth glance at the clock, she was rewarded by the sound of their car in the driveway. She took a deep breath and ran to open the door. A slim, rather tall girl with long red hair jumped out of the passenger side.

"Hi! Are you my Auntie Ede?"

Eden smiled and held out her arms.

"I sure am! Come and have a cuddle!"

She was moved to tears as the child ran towards her and flung out her arms. Eden scooped Shannon up in a warm embrace and kissed the top of her head.

"It's so lovely to see you!" She wiped her eyes with the back of one hand. "The last time I saw you, you had not long been born!"

She waved at Billy, and then with Shannon's hand in hers they walked into the hallway. Billy closed the door behind them, and for a moment Eden was lost for anything more to say. She held Shannon's gaze and smiled until the child spoke in a high excited voice.

"You look different to the photos in Mum's album."

Eden chuckled.

"I'm probably about twelve or thirteen years older than those photos now. My hair's a bit greyer, but I'm still *me*."

Shannon nodded.

"Why didn't you ever come with Uncle...er... Dad to visit me?"

"It's not that I didn't want to see you. Believe me, I *did*." Eden sighed. "Your mother and I don't speak to each other, and so that's why I've never gone with Dad to your house."

"Do I call you *Dad*?" Shannon regarded Billy with interest. "I don't know *what* to call you now."

Billy ruffled the top of his daughter's head.

"Just call me *Billy*."

"Why didn't you ever tell me that you were my dad?"

"Because your mum didn't want me to, and she's your legal parent." Billy replied with a shrug. "Come on, let's go and sit down."

Eden walked towards the front room and sank gratefully into an armchair. She was amazed to see that the child actually did slightly resemble Billy now that she had grown older. The two took seats side by side on the settee. She took a deep breath and composed herself.

"I remember your brothers. They were about eight when I last saw them."

Shannon pulled a face.

"They're my *half*-brothers now. They're at university. No-one's who they say they are anymore."

"They're still your brothers, no matter what." Eden replied gently. "What are they studying?"

"Er... I don't know." Shannon shrugged. "Something to do with engines. They want to help Dad, I mean...*the other Dad* and *my* dad in the scrapyard."

"Perhaps call him Aron so we don't get mixed up." Eden suggested." Hey ... I made a chocolate cake if you'd like some?"

She was pleased to see the girl's favourable reaction.

"Ooh, great! Can I have a bit please? Mum doesn't like me eating too much chocolate. She says it'll make me fat."

"Me too please." Billy piped up. "I don't *care* how fat I get."

Eden laughed and stood up.

"Shannon, come out to the kitchen with me and you can cut yourself a piece. I'll make a cup of tea and then we can take some in for Billy."

"How about you?" Shannon jumped to her feet. "Aren't you going to eat any?"

"Yes, I will." Eden nodded. "I felt a bit sick earlier on, but I'm all right now."

She held out her hand and the child grabbed it. Eden felt happier than she had in a long, long time. It seemed strange to have a child in the house, but she was going to enjoy Shannon's presence for as long as she was allowed to.

She feasted her eyes on the girl as she cut a rather large piece of cake. She had a sudden image of the pair of them shopping together and enjoying long girly chats. Could she call Shannon her step-daughter after all this time? Eden wondered what she had done to deserve such unaccustomed good luck.

Chapter Fifty One

Shannon wiped her mouth carefully with a serviette and smiled at her aunt and Billy.

"That was great. I love beef burgers and chips. Mum doesn't eat meat anymore, and so most of the time we *all* end up not having any."

"You can have meat anytime you like when you come to visit us here."

Shannon smiled at Eden.

"Great! Can I live with you two? It's better here than at home. Mum and me argue all the time, and Aron doesn't care about me at all."

She saw the quick glance flit between her aunt and Billy, and looked expectedly at them both. She felt a stab of dismay when Billy shook his head.

"You can visit any weekend you like, but your home during the week is with your mum and Aron and your brothers."

She wanted to cry with disappointment.

"I won't cause any trouble...I *promise.*"

Eden shook her head.

"Sorry, but you can visit any Friday night you like, if your mother permits, and stay until Billy takes you home on the Sunday evening. Of course, once you reach eighteen you can come and see us whenever you like, as you'll be an adult. I work every day at the library except Wednesdays and Sundays and so you'd be here on your own otherwise, but if you want to you can help me choose a colour to paint our spare room, so that we can turn it into your bedroom. I can order a duvet cover for the bed, and curtains to match. Nobody else will stay there, only *you*."

"All right." Shannon sighed. "I like pink."

"Then pink it shall be." Eden replied. "Would you like some jelly and custard? I've got strawberry or raspberry jelly."

"Yes please." Shannon nodded. "Strawberry."

She ate contentedly. Her aunt seemed normal enough. She had no idea why her mother had never made up with her sister, but right at this moment she didn't care. She would be able to twist her aunt and Billy around her little finger to get what she wanted. When she was able to stay in her new bedroom she knew what she would have to do… she would lock herself in and *refuse* to go home. Who in their right mind would want to live with people who lied all the time?

"When will my bedroom be ready?"

"Soon." Eden laughed. "Very soon."

"Can I have your mobile number?" Shannon took a phone out of her pocket. "I've got Billy's but I haven't got yours. We can text each other."

Eden, pleased at the outcome of the visit, fetched a pen and paper.

"Of course. I'll write it down for you."

***

The barrage of questions hit her like a ton of bricks as soon as Billy had reversed out of the driveway.

"What did you think of your aunt Eden?"

Shannon looked at her mother.

"She's lovely. I'm going to help her to decorate my bedroom there."

"Your *bedroom*?" Esme closed the front door. "What do you mean?"

"Billy and Aunt Ede said I can stay there at weekends."

"Oh, *did* they?"

"Yeah!" Shannon replied forcibly. "They did."

"What did she give you to eat?"

"Beefburgers, chips, chocolate cake and jelly."

"Good God! You know how we feel about meat!"

"Yeah." Shannon shrugged. "But *I* like it. Why do we have to eat what *you* like all the time?"

"What did she say about *me*?"

Shannon looked at her mother in disgust and started for the stairs.

"She says you won't speak to her."

"That's a lie!" Esme shouted to Shannon's retreating back. "It's *her* who won't speak to *me*!"

Shannon leaned over the upper landing bannisters.

"*Whatever!*"

She sighed, stomped into her bedroom, and slammed the door. *Grown-ups were worse than children sometimes!*

Chapter Fifty Two

Every day she dreaded her daughter's return from school, when the tears and tantrums would begin soon after Shannon stepped off the school bus and burst through the front door. Esme, grateful that Aron's *'I-told-you-so'* moment of triumph had so far failed to materialise, hated the fact that her husband might have been correct all along; *she should have told Shannon about Billy sooner*...

She looked up at the clock. Any minute now the bus would arrive at its designated stop, and then there would be just two more days of peace until the autumn term came to an end. Esme put the door on the latch and looked out into a gloomy street. Daylight had started to fade already, and a chilly December wind stirred up remnants of a pile of leaves she had raked up in the front garden. She pushed the front door to, turned up the hall thermostat, and made her way to the kitchen to begin preparations for a nut roast.

It was only after she had gathered together all the ingredients that she realised she had not been disturbed by Shannon's arrival. Esme wondered if her daughter had sneaked up the stairs while she had been busy in the kitchen. A quick but fruitless search of the house confirmed that the child had not come home at all.

Esme, worried now, picked up her mobile phone and dialled Shannon's number.

"What?"

She felt immediate relief to hear the moody voice on the other end of the line. Esme kept her voice light and steady.

"Hi. I just wondered where you are."

A radio played in the background. Esme decided not to catastrophise and instead to wait for her daughter's explanation.

"I phoned Aunty Eden at lunchtime. She doesn't work on Wednesdays. She said I could go to her house for tea, so she picked me up from school."

"But you should have told me!" Esme briefly closed her eyes against a rising anger. "Please don't do that again!"

"Do what? Not tell you or not go to Aunty Eden's?"

Esme wondered how long she could hold her temper.

"You must tell me where you're going if you get invited for tea and don't get on the school bus."

"I forgot."

"I'll come and get you *now*. You're not swanning off here there and everywhere without me knowing where you are!"

The line went dead. Esme emitted a scream of frustration then gathered up her bag and car keys.

***

It had been far too long since she had been at her sister's house. Esme turned into Valley Road with memories of happier Christmases with her extended family running through her mind. As she pulled up outside the house, she could see lights twinkling on a tree placed centre stage in the front bay window, and the room behind decorated with tinsel and holly.

A sudden bout of nerves prevented her from getting out of the car. Instead she dialled the landline number she still remembered off by heart.

"Hello?"

Of course, her sister wouldn't have been given her new mobile number. Esme swallowed a lump in her throat.

"It's Esme. I'm outside. I've come to collect Shannon."

"Okay. Sorry about this. She told me she'd already spoken to you about it."

"Well, she hadn't." Esme replied with a sigh. "Please let me know if she does this again."

"Yes, I will. She's eating a sandwich at the moment. Do you want to come in and wait?"

"Er…if that's okay?"

"Sure. Come up to the door and I'll let you in."

Her heart started up a faster rhythm in her chest. Esme climbed out of the driver's seat and opened the garden gate just as Eden pulled back the front door. She was surprised to see how grey her sister's hair had become in the intervening years. Eden looked stolidly middle aged now, and Esme tried hard not to stare.

"Hi. Sorry to bother you."

She felt awkward and eager to be away. Relieved to see a smile on her sister's face, she stood awkwardly in the hallway and clutched her bag as though her life depended on it.

"It's no bother. Come into the kitchen. Shannon's nearly finished."

The house was not familiar to her anymore. Esme checked her surroundings; there was a large conservatory off the kitchen where a patio had once stood, and the old kitchen units she remembered had been ripped out. She ignored the look of venom on her daughter's face and instead turned towards Eden.

"Thanks for picking Shannon up, but please phone me next time if this happens again. If you have your phone handy I'll let you have my new number."

"Okay." Eden rummaged in her bag and brought out an iPhone. "Fire away. I'll give you *my* new mobile number as well."

As they swapped contact details, out of the corner of her eye she saw that Shannon had risen from her seat intent on making her way out of the room. Esme placed herself squarely in the doorway.

"Home, Madam. We're going home *now.*"

Shannon, slim and lithe, dodged under Esme's arm and ran full pelt up the stairs.

"I'm staying here with Aunty Eden! She doesn't lie to me!"

Esme heard the sound of a key in the lock and sighed.

"I'll have to get Aron to come round later and sort her out. I'm the Wicked Witch of the East at the moment. Sorry to put you out for a few more hours."

"It's no trouble." Eden shrugged. "I'll give her some dinner later."

Esme nodded, embarrassed that her sister had witnessed her lack of control over Shannon. She swallowed a twinge of jealousy and hurried towards the front door.

"Thanks."

She could hardly wait to get back in her car and drive away.

Chapter Fifty Three

Aron's face fell as Billy opened the front door and shook his head.

"When I said you were on your way round, she ran and locked herself in the bedroom again. She's had some dinner, so hunger won't bring her out."

"Shit." Aron sighed. "Look, I'll get you a new door if I have to kick it down."

"Let's hope it won't come to that. Drill out the lock instead, eh?"

Aron made straight for the stairs.

"I'll go up and see what I can do."

He followed the sound of a TV towards a newly painted hardwood door bearing the sign '*Shannon's Room*'. He took a deep breath and rapped on one of the upper panels with his knuckles.

"Shannon, it's Dad. It's time to go home."

Canned laughter from the TV increased in volume. Aron, irritated beyond measure, thumped again on the door with a fist.

"Shannon! Can you hear me?"

Sound from the TV became deafening.

"Come out *now*! If you don't, this door's coming off!"

He gave the wood an experimental kick for good measure. A scream erupted from within.

"I'm staying here with my real dad!"

A more forceful kick buckled the frame. Behind him he heard Eden and Billy run up the stairs. Inside the bedroom Shannon's screams belted out a discordant duet with the TV.

"I'll put it right for you." Aron, panting, turned to Billy. "I'm not letting an eleven year old kid get the better of *me*."

"Let me speak to her." Eden pushed forward. "She might listen to me."

"She's past that." Aron held out one hand. "You're wasting your time."

"Shannon, it's Aunty Eden. Come out love, eh?"

"No!"

Aron cursed under his breath and motioned for Eden to move away from the door. With another well-aimed kick at the lock, the framework gave way. Aron, with Eden and Billy close behind, rushed through the door. Aron caught hold of Shannon's arm with one hand, and with his daughter kicking and screaming in protest he made his way over to the TV and turned it off. Slightly breathless, he looked at her.

"*I* am the parent, and *you* are the child. You will do as I say! Billy, I'll be back later on to repair the door."

"You're *not* my dad! I *won't* do as you say!"

With some difficulty he manoeuvred a wild-eyed Shannon out of the door, still kicking. When she dropped to her knees at the foot of the stairs Aron could take no more. Impatient to be gone, he cursed again, hoisted her up in a fireman's lift, and carried her screaming over his shoulder down the stairs and out to the car.

***

"Whatever have you done to her? She's like a wild animal!"

Aron, with Shannon encased in a vice-like grip, ignored Esme's look of disgust. He dodged a kick from Shannon, and then deposited her sobbing on the doorstep.

"She has to learn who's boss around here. If she thinks she can rule the roost, she's got another think coming. I'm going back to Billy's. I had to kick down the bedroom door to get her out, so now I've got to go and repair the bloody thing. She's more trouble than both the boys put together! She's already had dinner, so *bath and bed*. I don't care if it *is* only eight o'clock."

Impervious to the neighbours' stares, he turned around then walked to the car and drove off at breakneck speed.

Chapter Fifty Four

"Come on love, let's go in and you can have a nice hot bath."

Esme put her arm around her daughter's shoulders. For once Shannon, still weeping, offered no resistance.

"Was Dad a bit heavy-handed with you?"

She closed the front door behind them and felt Shannon's arms go around her middle.

"He..he's not my dad!"

Anxious to avoid a fresh bout of weeping, Esme remained silent and cuddled Shannon in the hallway until her sobbing had ceased.

"He may not be your dad, but he loves you just as much as he does the boys."

With her head against Esme's chest, Shannon's muffled reply was just about audible.

"I want to live with my *real* dad, the one I was supposed to live with in the first place."

Esme's heart sank at her daughter's words, but decided the best thing was to play along and hope it was a passing fancy.

"Okay you know your dad, but you haven't known your Aunty Ede long enough. How d'you *know* you'd like to live with her?"

"*She* wouldn't keep making me do stuff I don't want to do."

"Is that so?" Esme held Shannon at arm's length and glanced down at her. "Well, the only thing to be done then is for me to speak to your aunt and see what she says."

She ignored the startled look of surprise on her daughter's face and carried on.

"And as I've already told you, you'll have to change schools. Is that okay with you?"

"No."

"Well, you can't have it all your own way. Perhaps you can stay with them during some of the school holidays instead, and still go to the same school. How about that?"

She was rewarded with a smile, a hiccup and a nod.

"Good." Esme replied. "I'll have to speak to Eden then, as she'll need to take time off work."

As she followed her daughter upstairs, Esme mused on the fact that she had now made initial contact with her sister again after eleven years of silence. Perhaps something good had come out of Shannon's tantrums after all.

***

"Hi, it's Esme".

She felt relief at her sister's lack of surprise.

"Oh, hi. Is Shannon okay now?"

"Yes, sorry about your door."

Eden chuckled.

"Oh that's okay, Aron's fixing it."

"Er…I've been having a chat with Shannon. She would like to spend some of the school holidays with you. I don't know how you'd feel about that, as obviously you'd have to take time off work."

There was a pause as her sister digested the information. Esme continued.

"Of course if you don't want the responsibility, just say…"

"We'd love to have her stay." Eden replied. "I'm just a bit choked up. I-I've waited a long time for this."

Tears stung the back of Esme's eyes.

"We're going to Aron's parents for Christmas, but I'm going to do a buffet for the twenty seventh. Would you and Billy like to come? The boys will be home, and I'll ask Mum and Dad and Pamela as well."

"Yes, that sounds lovely." Eden sniffed. "I'd like that."

Esme ended the call and burst into tears.

***

She looked over at the bedside clock as Aron slipped into bed beside her.

"You've been a long time."

"I had to mend the frame." Aron yawned. "Then Billy and I had a couple of beers. Ede says you've invited them here on the twenty seventh."

"Yeah." She snuggled up against him.

"What's brought this on?"

"Oh, I thought it was time we buried the hatchet. Shannon wants to spend some of the school holidays with them. I think it's only fair really. I've been a selfish bitch over the years. She's growing up, and she's got a mind of her own."

"She sure has." Aron laughed. "She's got a mean kick as well."

"Thanks for not saying *I told you so*."

"What's the point?" Aron replied. "It won't change the past."

Esme reached up and kissed his cheek.

"No, we can't change it, I know, but I *can* do something about the future, and I will. *We* will, won't we Aron?"

"Yeah, I will." Aron nodded. "If *you* can do it, then so can I. It's taken me all this time to realise I need to be a father to Shannon, just as much as Billy does. Hell, I don't want my kids to hate me."

Esme let a momentary wave of pleasure wash over her. It had cost Aron eleven wasted years to accept her daughter, and as far as she was concerned things from now on could only get better.

Chapter Fifty Five

Aron knocked lightly on his daughter's door.

"Can I come in?"

He was relieved when the bedroom door opened a fraction and Shannon's head peeped round.

"Hi. Sorry I kicked you yesterday."

"That's okay. I'll forgive you if you forgive me."

She smiled and opened the door fully, and he followed her in. He stood there momentarily looking about the room, aware with a painful stab of shame that his surroundings were not too familiar.

"Wow, you've won lots of merits at school!"

"I've got a new one." Shannon reached into her school bag. "I haven't put it on the wall yet. This one's for French."

Aron studied the merit award intently.

"How about we go and celebrate that you're doing so well at school? If you like we can go to the dry ski slope at Ipswich. I've never been skiing before, but I'm game if *you* are."

"Cool!" Shannon clapped her hands. "Ellie and Marie have been there!"

"We can have a lesson first from one of the instructors. I'll book it up then?"

"Yes please! Er... Dad..."

Aron smiled at Shannon.

"What?"

"I don't know what to call you now. Aunty Eden said it might be a good idea to call you Aron? Not many kids have two dads, and I'm confused."

"Hmm...you're right." Aron considered for a moment. "You can either call us both *Dad*, or you can call us by our names. I don't mind ...whatever you want is okay by me."

"I'll call you *Dad* then, because I've always called you *Dad*. It'll seem funny calling you *Aron*."

Aron felt at a loss for words. He needed to be the best father that he could be to the child standing before him, a child willing to still call him *Dad* despite his previous shortcomings in the parenthood department. He needed to show an interest in her life before he lost her for good. He suddenly looked forward to learning how to ski.

***

"Dad, you're doing it wrong!" Shannon threw back her head with laughter. "You need to put your toes in the ski first and then the rest of your foot!"

Aron, still smarting from spending upwards of £100 on lessons and ski hire, brought his mind away from his wallet to where Shannon stood ready to go with Dave, the instructor.

"Whoops, I wasn't listening."

He returned a thin smile from Dave with one of his own. Dave glared at him before continuing.

"We're going to glide along using one ski and two poles, and then we'll use two skis."

Kids 30 years younger than him were whizzing down the slope at a rate of knots. Aron wished he were back in the scrapyard doing what he knew how to do best, but it was time to suck up his embarrassment and bond with his daughter.

"Gotcha."

He grinned at Shannon and moved forward on the ski, all the time wondering how Eddie the Eagle ever managed a 90 metre jump. His right knee protested at his new and unfamiliar posture. His lower back set up an ache to rival the one taking place in his knee.

"This is cool, Dad!" Shannon's red hair flew behind her. "I'm going faster than you!"

Aron pushed himself along, feeling about as nimble as a ten ton elephant.

"Because you're lighter, probably."

To his annoyance, Shannon arrived back at base slightly sooner.

"Can we use two skis now, Dave?"

The moment he had dreaded was upon him. Aron clicked his foot into the second ski and grabbed both poles. To his annoyance, Dave looked him up and down.

"Don't forget to stand upright and slightly forward, and bend your knees a bit. We'll go along the flat, and then I'll show you how to move uphill."

Aron gave Shannon a wink as his resentment towards Dave grew with every passing moment.

"Enjoying yourself?"

"Yeah, thanks Dad."

He hated the feeling of being out of control. Aron lumbered behind Shannon with a maniacal grin on his face.

"You're too quick for me. I can't catch up."

Dave glided effortlessly past.

"Ski up to the bottom of the slope, then turn sideways to climb up, one step with the right foot, and then bring the left foot up next to it. Press down with the poles and stop in the middle of the slope then turn and watch how I come to a halt at the bottom by turning the ends of the skis slightly inwards."

He kept pace with Shannon, moving gracelessly sideways up the slope. His right knee screamed a chorus or two. He gritted his teeth.

"I'm really getting the hang of this!"

"Can we come again, Dad?" Shannon laughed and moved upwards. "This is the best day ever!"

It was worth putting his middle aged body through the torture just to see her happy. Aron held up his stick in agreement. *Would the guilt ever go away?* He had resented her from the get-go, but the kid had not asked to be born. Aron smiled at her. For all he knew she might even be the comfort of his old age.

"Sure. Just let me get today over with first."

He lifted his poles and let the skis take him down the slope.

Chapter Fifty Six - Epilogue

The long trestle table groaned with Christmas fare. Esme squeezed a tube of Pringles in the last space and stepped back.

"There, it's all done. That should be enough. They'll be here in a minute."

"Can I start now?" James grabbed a sausage roll. "I'm starving."

"Ah, no, not yet!" Esme slapped his behind. "Don't take any more!"

Jared's hand reached tentatively across the table.

"If he's got one, then *I* want one."

"Oh, for God's sake!" Esme laughed. "Take one and go away!"

Momentarily startled as the doorbell rang, Esme ran out of the dining room and along the hallway. She smoothed her hair with one hand and then opened the door as Shannon rushed down the stairs.

"Merry Christmas!"

"And to you!" Billy stepped inside and kissed her cheek. "I've brought a crowd with me."

She looked beyond him to where Eden stood awkwardly in the porch with their parents. She waved at Donna, Steve and Pamela standing behind them.

"Come in all of you, don't stand out there in the cold!"

"Hi Ez. We come bearing gifts."

Eden came towards her, and she felt the warmth of her sister's embrace. As she returned the hug with one of her own, she heard the twins start up a round of applause. Esme grinned as the rest of the family joined in.

"I haven't earned that at all, but we're going to make up for lost time, aren't we Ede?"

"We sure are." Eden nodded.

"Yeah!" Shannon jumped up and down. "This is cool! I've got *two* mums and *two* dads!"

James ruffled the top of Shannon's head.

"And two brothers!"

Her entire family stood around her in the hallway. Esme smiled and knew that Christmas 2019 would be the best ever. There had been talk of a new virus that had erupted in China on the news, but that was thousands of miles away and she was not going to worry about it just at that moment. She had her sister back, and that was all that mattered. Aron and Shannon were getting on like a house on fire, especially after the appearance of two child-size skis on Christmas Day, and so the virus could go and take a long running 90 metre jump.

THE END

If you have enjoyed this story, you may also like '*The Donor*', another family drama also by Stevie Turner. You can find out more about '*The Donor*' by visiting www.stevie-turner-author.co.uk

OTHER BOOKS BY STEVIE TURNER

THE PILATES CLASS
A HOUSE WITHOUT WINDOWS
FOR THE SAKE OF A CHILD
LILY: A SHORT STORY
NO SEX PLEASE, I'M MENOPAUSAL!
A RATHER UNUSUAL ROMANCE
THE DAUGHTER-IN-LAW SYNDROME
REVENGE
THE NOISE EFFECT
CRUISING DANGER
THE DONOR
REPENT AT LEISURE
LIFE: 18 SHORT STORIES
ALYS IN HUNGERLAND
MIND GAMES
LEG-LESS AND CHALAZA
PARTNERS IN TIME
FINDING DAVID: A PARANORMAL SHORT STORY
EXAMINING KITCHEN CUPBOARDS

Website: http://www.stevie-turner-author.co.uk/

Twitter: https://twitter.com/StevieTurner6

Blog: https://steviet3.wordpress.com/

Google:
https://plus.google.com/u/0/105747643789021738179/posts/p/pub

Pinterest: https://uk.pinterest.com/stevieturner988/

Amazon Author Page: http://www.amazon.co.uk/Stevie-Turner/e/B00AV7YOTU/

Email: stevie@stevie-turner-author.co.uk

Goodreads:
https://www.goodreads.com/author/show/7172051.Stevie_Turner

YouTube:
https://www.youtube.com/channel/UClWFuLQHDqGmOM3KbKJ-Z0g

www.ingramcontent.com/pod-product-compliance
Lightning Source LLC
Chambersburg PA
CBHW051434170626
46809CB00006B/2461